Nikoline Kaiser
THE DREAMING OF MAN
Neon Hemlock Press

NEON HEMLOCK

Neon Hemlock Press
www.neonhemlock.com
@neonhemlock

The Dreaming of Man
Nikoline Kaiser

Cover Illustration and Title by J.J. Epping
Interior Design and Layout by dave ring
Edited by dave ring

Print ISBN-13: 978-1-966503-09-5
Ebook ISBN-13: 978-1-966503-10-1

THE DREAMING OF MAN

NIKOLINE KAISER

For Gina

*It is the bloody business which informs
Thus to mine eyes. Now o'er the one-half world
Nature seems dead, and wicked dreams abuse
The curtained sleep.*
—Macbeth, *Act 2, Scene 1*

THERE IT WAS, one sunny morning; a letter waiting for him on the breakfast table, his landlady, Mrs. Danson, bustling around with food and tea. It was a slim, unassuming thing, resting against the small bowl of milk that she always filled in the mornings, though neither of them took milk with their tea.

Lawrence had not received any sort of correspondence in a while; his academy fellows were all here in the city with him—prone to sending small notes, though more in danger of simply showing up as they wished—and his family had long since stopped writing, with the exception of his uncle, James. So it was with some surprise that Lawrence picked up the slim envelope, and was unable to recognize the writing, nor the return-address on it.

"Mrs. Danson? Who left this?"

She tipped more tea into his cup, though it was already overflowing. "Oh, some young boy. Didn't get a good look at his face. Do you want sugar in this, dear?"

"No…no, thank you…" Lawrence was wholly distracted, not noticing the *plop* as Mrs. Danson dropped his customary three sugars into the tea. He had opened the letter and been met with a wind of smells: sea-salt and sea-weed and—it had been so long since he had been to the sea, he recalled. A lifetime ago. Quite a different life, back then. But who would be writing to him from the seaside?

Honorable Doctor Cooper
We beseech you now… town of Osmund… terrible disease… striking the young ones in particular… your old friend, Mr. Henry Burkley… funeral arrangements… no living relative…

And there, started in the middle of the page and repeated by the very end: the simple word *please*. A doctor's summoning.

The letter was unsigned, and Lawrence might have thought the whole thing a distasteful joke if not for the extreme sincerity behind the words, if not for the fact that Henry had left to go doctoring in smaller towns. It was to fulfill their shared dreams of helping those who might not otherwise afford or have their services at the ready. Henry had been brave enough to do what Lawrence had always wanted—and now it seemed he had paid for it with his life.

His hands shook as he put down the letter. His eyes found Mrs. Danson's, saw her staring quite stricken at him. Whatever look was on his face, it was bad enough to have made her forget completely about their morning-tea.

"I think I have to go pack a bag," he said. His cup rattled as he tried to lift it with a shaking hand, tea spilling over into the saucer, clumps of undissolved sugar staining the porcelain.

OSMUND TRULY WAS a wretched town—that was all Lawrence could think, as he stepped out of the carriage that had brought him there. The ocean and sky were both gray, and the faint rays of sunlight that peeked through seemed to do so only as a cursory nod to the scant vegetation that grew around here. Over Osmund, the sun shone as a chore before it did so as a joy.

He had not exactly expected a welcoming party, not at this hour of the evening, but the complete void of people in the town square sent a chill down his spine. The buildings around him held only a few lighted windows and the entire place was eerily silent, as if even the mice were holding their breath. If he strained his ears, he could faintly hear the sound of waves from the ocean, just beyond the square. A wooden sign swung back and forth over what was clearly the sole inn of the town, though it was too dark for him to make out the words.

It swung wilder as the door beneath it was slammed open; Lawrence could not help himself, but startled with a yelp, clutching at his medical bag.

The man who walked out of the inn was thin, and so pale that he seemed like a spectre appearing from the gray shadows around him. He was tall—Lawrence, a rather short man himself, thought this man would be tall even had he been surrounded by giants. The man had to duck his head to not hit it against the door-frame. His hands were large, old and wiry, but strong. He wore a dirty apron over simple clothes, and his eyes seemed to shine in the gloom around them.

"Doctor Cooper?" the man asked, with a pleasant voice that seemed to leap through the quiet, a snake striking forth.

"I am he."

The man smiled at him, teeth pearly-white. He moved his hand, but it was only to wipe it on his apron; Lawrence's own aborted attempt at a handshake went ignored.

"I am Reverend Nathaniel Richards. Most folks here just call me Richards or Rev. I run the inn, too. I'm pleased you got my letter, very pleased."

"Oh. I had not realized you sent it. There was no signature."

Reverend Richards cocked his head to the side, eyes wide. "Truly? I must have forgotten. My apologies, you must have been dreadfully confused. Come in, come inside, please. The weather is awful outside."

Indeed, a fine sheen of rain had started to fall, but even walking inside and taking off his coat, Lawrence could still feel the chill. It seemed to cling to the wall, and even the warm glow of the fireplace in the corner could not chase it out.

The inn held only a few lanterns, leaving most of the interior cast in shadow; it had two other patrons, a pair of fishermen by the looks of it. One still wore his coat, a huge thing that seemed to swallow him whole; it spilled like ink over his shoulders and down the bench he was seated on. He was smoking away on a new-looking pipe, the smoke curling up and making the air heavy. Across from him sat a youngster, pockmarks on his sallow face, his hair almost as fiery red as Lawrence's own. Both looked up as he entered, their gazes curious, steely. They were assessing him, Lawrence felt, and he straightened his back in response. He had not survived university and the big city to be cowed by anyone who looked at him sideways.

"Settle down, boys," Richards said. "The doctor is here."

The pair did not quite relax, but some of the tension left their shoulders.

The younger one spoke: "My name's Marlyn. This one's Thompson."

Lawrence did not know if that was a last or first name, but he did not care to ask. He gave the two a nod in return, and followed the Reverend through a door behind the bar and into a small room. Fairly secluded, Richards hauled two chairs together by a small table.

"Here, put your bags down, and your coat. You must be exhausted, but I suspect you won't sleep until I've answered some questions."

"I would prefer that, yes," Lawrence said. Even so, he waited patiently while Richards put his things away and poured a mug of something hot and steaming for them both.

"Here, this'll warm you up. Now, where to start."

"Henry…with Doctor Berkeley, please."

"Yes, yes, of course. A tragic thing."

"You said in the letter that he drowned?"

Richards nodded. "It happens, unfortunately. We've had so much rain and the dock gets slippery with it. We'd had, well…it was rather our fault, old Thompson back there was convincing him to take the night off, he had been working so hard, truly, so hard. He was a blessing for this town. But the doctor was a bit in his cups and then suddenly he was just gone from the place and we didn't…

it took us a while to check the docks. His body had come up on the beach already, but it was too late."

Lawrence swallowed heavily, but when he opened his mouth he still had not found his voice. Richards was watching him carefully. Not knowing what else to do, he took a drink from the mug.

He almost spat it out again. He had expected tea, perhaps some form of grog, but he had no idea what this was. It tasted acrid, like brine and salt; he almost thought he could feel it, grinding between his teeth. He coughed, and set the mug back down.

Richards' eyes were glinting, knowing. Lawrence would not be so rude as to comment, or ask for something else to drink. At least Richards had been right about one thing— the drink warmed him, from his mouth all the way down to his belly. It also made his stomach turn and he was happy he had not eaten much today. He did not fancy throwing up all over his host, only minutes after meeting.

"You alright, doctor?"

"Yes." *Doctor.* Richards had called Henry *mister* in the letter, forgoing his proper title. But the man had also forgotten to sign his own name, so perhaps he really had been as confused as he claimed. That would also explain how incomprehensible his story was to someone who knew Henry. The man did not drink. And he was an excellent swimmer.

The warmth of the drink could not chase away the unsettling dread rising in Lawrence. It could be explained, of course—if Thompson, or whoever, really had pressured Henry to partake in drink, then he might be quite affected; enough to tumble off the docks and forget how to swim.

But then the letter, explaining so little of this. The letter, unsigned. It prickled at a memory, something Henry had once said to him, but Lawrence could not recall it now. He was tired—he was grieving. Henry was *dead* and now he had both read it and heard it, and yet it still did not feel real.

"Doctor Cooper?"

He shook his head, forcing himself back to the present. "I am sorry, Reverend. I am quite overcome with grief, it would seem. And confusion, as well. You said in your letter that you held the funeral here, that Henry is buried here?"

"Yes, that is so."

"Yet why was his family not contacted? They have their own burial grounds. They would want him back home."

Richards frowned. "To tell you the truth, we did not know. He expressed a wish to be buried here, and we rather thought to…that is, the boys wanted the funeral done and handled. Corpses tend to not last long if left out in the open."

Lawrence felt a sense of vertigo, almost tumbling to the floor. What did that even mean? *Not last?* Did they decay faster because of the brisk sea-air? Were the gulls and other water-fowls desperate for a taste of decaying human flesh?

"Richards, sir…I am afraid I have made a mistake." Something here was *wrong*, Lawrence had felt it from the moment he'd gotten the letter. But now he was sure, his instincts screaming at him to get away as quickly as possible. He had not survived this long, as who he was, by ignoring his instincts.

"Ah?" Richards did not seem particularly surprised by this; only disappointed. "Have I got the wrong man, then? Should I have contacted someone else?"

The way he said *wrong man* made Lawrence almost choke on his own breath. Suddenly the room around them felt altogether too small, and he became aware that the two other patrons had left without him noticing, and that the lanterns had grown dimmer. The rest of the flickering lights painted shadows on the shelves full of bottles, writhing, moving across dark-stained glass.

"Yes, absolutely. His family should have been contacted immediately." *I* should have done that, Lawrence realized, even as he said it. He should have let the Berkeley-family know, and he should not have gone here alone; only he had been so disoriented, so confused by it all. The letter had not even been signed, for God's sake, like some sort of bad hoax. Like the author had forgotten his own name. "I…I am sorry, but I must go…now…"

Richards rose with him, and his great height was almost enough to make Lawrence shrink back down. But no, no; he had made his decision.

"But, Doctor Cooper, you only just arrived…"

"I…I must insist, I am going now…I am leaving." He grabbed for his coat, but could not find it. That's right, Richards had taken it, put it…ah, there it was.

"Please, Doctor, it is night-time, it has already grown dark outside. Are you meaning to walk? We cannot get transportation for you…at least wait until the morning."

Lawrence went still. He took a deep breath. Yes. Of course, in the morning. He was panicking, and while he knew he was right to be skeptical of the whole situation, this was, perhaps, an overreaction. Even if it was not, Richards was watching him with shrewd eyes and Lawrence got the feeling he would not be well-pleased to put up with more antics. Lawrence was being an ungrateful guest.

"Of course, you're right. A room for the night, at the inn, would be…"

"Absolutely! I've already had our best place set aside for you. Ah, but I've forgotten the linens…I'll wake Josephine, here, wait here."

And he was off before Lawrence could think to protest. He was left alone, sitting behind the bar, vestiges of panic still in his throat. He rose slowly, glancing at the door. Richards had taken one of the lanterns with him, leaving the room was even darker. Outside, the rain had turned to hail, thundering against the roof.

Not quite knowing what possessed him to do so, Lawrence walked over to the door. He did not bring his coat or his bag, only himself, as he reached out slowly and pulled at the handle. Locked. It was locked. Of course it was.

Richards had not done it, so it must have been one of the other two men who had a key, who knew to lock the door when they walked out, because Lawrence would not be leaving tonight. Would Richards have ever let him? Even had it been feasible, if Lawrence had insisted, had said he would walk the miles and miles back to the city if that's what it took—would he have been allowed to go?

He returned to his things, reaching down to pick up his bags, sling his coat over his arms. He waited, quite patiently, his heart pounding with a frantic fervor, as two sets of footsteps came from upstairs and down towards him.

He saw Richards first, the man smiling wide, teeth bared in the dark. And behind him came what must be Josephine, a small girl of no more than fifteen, dark red hair in unruly braids, a simple robe thrown over her night-clothes. Lawrence frowned, but it was not until she stepped closer to the light of the lantern that he really saw her. That he recognized her.

"Hello, sir," she said, voice scratchy from sleep. "I'm Josephine. I'll just make up your bed for you."

All he could do was stare. Josephine blinked, some of her sleepiness fading.

"Doctor Cooper, sir?"

Lawrence opened his mouth, almost said *you look just like your*…but then he stopped himself. "Yes, hello. Hello. Hel—Josephine, was it?"

"Yes, sir."

His tongue was sticking to the roof of his mouth, dry as a bone. "Lawrence, if you please. You can call me Lawrence."

She gave him a strange look. Lawrence was aware, as if from far away, that Richards was regarding him with a knowing expression. He could not tear his eyes away.

"Alright, then. Right this way, doctor. I'll show you to your room."

THE ROOM ITSELF was well-furnished, with a bed holding a surprisingly soft mattress, a writing desk, a wide dresser and even a small bookshelf, which, however, held nothing but a Bible and a truly hefty volume of the collected works of Shakespeare.

Despite the lovely mattress, Lawrence did not sleep one wink. A storm howled outside, battering against the window. He was painfully aware of the other souls in the inn, of Richards who was sleeping down the hall, and of Josephine, who had pointed to her shoe-closet of a room on the floor above his, and said to come knocking if he needed anything.

"I've a lock on my door, though," she had said, as soon as Richards was out of earshot. "So don't try anything."

Lawrence spluttered briefly, but then calmed himself. Smart girl. "I would not, but I am glad you are taking measures. Let me ask, is there a lock on *my* door?"

She gave him a look that was achingly familiar; he could have sworn he saw her lips twitch. "Yes. But I have the key to it, and so does the Reverend."

"Anyone else?"

Again, that look, almost of recognition. As if they could see each other. "Marlyn gets in wherever he wants," she said. "He's a sneak, but he's harmless."

Lawrence hoped that was true. "Right. Thank you."

She hesitated in the doorway. He would recognize the oval shape of her face everywhere, and even paired with her broad nose, her dark eyes, so unlike…yes, this was a face he would know if he was dead and gone, a face that proved a merging of two others, with traces of something unique, something wholly her. She had broken her nose once, he noted, a light swing in it, towards the left, barely discernible. She had freckles, too, though they were barely visible against her tan skin.

Lawrence could almost convince himself that it was a coincidence. That surely, out in the world, there existed a list of features and as they were assigned, through genes and pure happenstance, there existed people so similar, perhaps even identical, to someone you already knew—even if those people had not a speck of blood shared between them. That had to be it, he thought, a little hysterically. That had to be it, because it couldn't be…

"I liked Henry," Josephine had said to him, before they parted for sleep. "He was kinder to me than anyone's been since my pa died." *Dead, then. He's dead.* "He didn't drink, he hated the stuff. He hated the docks more, he never went down there. Said the ocean scared him, even if he could swim."

Lawrence's panic had receded, inch by inch. He looked at the girl then, not as a shocking specter or reminder, but as…as…a potential ally. Her brown eyes held the light of intelligence, but they also held a vulnerable trust, the kind Lawrence knew he himself had leveled Henry with, once upon a time.

"I know," he'd said. "Anything you can tell me…"

There was a *thump*, from further down the hall, as if someone was getting in or out of bed. "But we can talk in the morning, yes? When the sun is up."

Josephine had made a sound that might have been a snort of laughter. "That's the thing, doctor," she said. "Sun doesn't rise over Osmund. But I'll see you in the morning."

LAWRENCE DID NOT get one wink of sleep, though as the night progressed, he found himself deeper and deeper in the dream-like land of memories. Memories of the last time he had gotten drunk—well and truly the last time—and spilled his guts to Henry, shed the skin from himself until he had been laid bare beneath that scrutinizing gaze. He had woken the next morning expecting condemnation, perhaps even public execution, but all Henry had was a glass of water and a thousand questions for him, intrigued rather than repulsed. Lawrence could count on one hand the number of people who had accepted the truth of who he was; his uncle had, facing rejection from the rest of the family, and Lawrence suspected that Mrs. Danson knew more than she had ever let on, and then there was…there was Josephine's father.

Two of those people were dead now, he recalled with a dull thud of grief. Unless he was mistaken about Josephine, and she had no relation…

He turned over on his side, shivering with the cold. His one taste of Richards' concoction had left him dizzy once the warmth from it had disappeared. Whatever had been in it, he vowed to never have as much of a sip again.

Another memory rose, of Henry ranting on, jumping from one scientific subject to the other, until suddenly it was no longer scientific but pure fantasy—strange dreams of a red moon etched permanent onto the sky, of beasts rising from the sea, great as mountains, coming to wipe mankind from the face of the Earth.

Lawrence had laughed, but Henry had seemed quite earnest in parts of his story, even as he had smiled and dismissed the theories himself. He had spoken of the finer details too, of how one might recognize the signs of such creatures, like trails of dust left behind in a messy man's wake.

Let me guess, Lawrence had said, in a mood to tease his old friend. *They write with their left hand, if they can write at all. Diabolical little devils. Oh, and when you take their clothes off, it's never what you expect beneath!* He'd raised his own left hand, his writing hand, and swatted at Henry.

Lawrence turned in the bed again, frowning. Half-asleep, what Henry had said slipped away from him. *Unease.* That had been it, but unease could be so many things. Lawrence felt uneasy when a dog barked too loudly, yet he doubted they were all some ill-begotten creature from the deep sea. They had spoken of names too, but that talk had been different—the manner of choosing a name for oneself, of changing what you were called as a way to change yourself. How you could run from some things, yet not others. How a man, in the end, was little more than a name on a piece of paper, once his body and spirit were gone from this earth.

That had not been Henry's warning; he had said something else. It was almost morning before Lawrence could hear his voice again:

Something will be wrong, Henry had said. *Something will be wrong, but you will not know what it is, only that it is* wrong.

OSEPHINE HAD BEEN right. When Lawrence came to the next morning, only faint light fell in through the windows. He got up slowly, feeling wrong-footed, his head pounding with pain. It always did when he got too little sleep, but today seemed particularly bad. He washed his face and made sure the door was locked before he changed into fresh clothes. From his bag he took the things he could not leave behind—his journal, keys to the house, the small knife his uncle had once gifted him—and put them in the pockets of his coat, which he put over one arm. He walked downstairs slowly; the air was heavy with the lanterns and the fire lit anew, to chase away the gloom and cold of morning.

Reverend Richards was already awake, eating porridge and drinking more of what appeared to be the warm concoction from yesterday. He smiled when he saw Lawrence, and motioned for him to come sit.

Josephine flickered in and out of view, finally emerging from the kitchen to put a bowl of gray sludge—the aforementioned porridge—in front of Lawrence. Despite the unappetizing sight, he thanked her kindly.

"Sit down, dear girl," Richards said. "There's no other guests now. Grab a bowl, I know you haven't eaten."

Lawrence was struck by the kind look on the man's face, a contrast to the sly cunning he thought he'd seen yesterday. Josephine hesitated, before she did as bid; to his surprise, she sat down next to him rather than the Reverend, her small form a warm spot by his side.

"There you are," said Richards. There was something very pleased in his expression, as his eyes went from one to the other. Lawrence concentrated on his porridge, relieved that it tasted at least a little less bland than it looked. They ate in silence, though Richards finished far before the rest of them. He seemed content to simply sit and look. It made Lawrence's skin crawl to have eyes on him, and he felt compelled to break the silence. He cast around for something to say, and then, because he had noted it, the one pleasant thing about this place: "You keep a clean house here."

Richards smiled. "That is all Josephine's doing. She's got an eye for proper hygiene, to the bafflement of most people here, I must say."

"To most people in most places," Lawrence said, unable to stop from sneaking a quick glance at Josephine. Her head was bowed, eyes fixed on her empty bowl. She had just one braid today, but most of her curls were escaping the twists and the tie. Looser curls than her father's had been, he recalled, but still a myriad of them, like a beautiful Medusa with her snakes. "I prefer a clean place as well. It has been a matter of contention between me and my patients, not to mention some of the other doctors."

He had no idea why he was sharing this much, but now Josephine's head was lifting so she could look at him.

"Keeping things clean is important," she said, though she seemed almost shy, as if afraid he would not agree. Lawrence found it easy to give her a smile.

"It is. It keeps one healthy. Time and again I seem to be proven correct in this, but many of my fellows still refuse to believe me."

Josephine picked at her nails—a bad habit he himself had developed when he was at university. Another pang to the heart. She did not say anything, but the faint set of her mouth hinted at a smile.

"Well." Richards pushed away from the table. "I have to tend to the church. Josephine, if you don't mind closing up the inn for now and taking Doctor Cooper to the cemetery? I believe he might like to pay his respects to his old friend."

Lawrence's mood instantly plummeted, his stomach churning at the thought of Henry buried *here*, in this sad, desolate place. But perhaps it was true what the Reverend had told him yesterday, that Henry had wished to be buried here. He'd dedicated his life to places like this and had been more than willing to live here, after all. Why not stay in perpetuity?

He helped Josephine in clearing the table, despite her protests, and he wiped it down under her discerning eye, well-pleased with himself when his cleaning came up to her standards. He put on his coat, making sure his things were still there, and followed her outside.

There were a few more people bustling about at this time, though the town was by no means busy. Most of them stopped to stare once they saw Lawrence, and he had to force himself to smile and greet them politely. *Be nice, be affable. Then they can accuse you of nothing, no matter what they think.* Only a handful greeted Josephine as she walked: an old, one-eyed woman who rather reminded him of Mrs. Danson, a young girl with hands full of weeds from her garden and Marlyn, who seemed to be skulking in the shadows by a small booth peddling fish.

Most others ignored her. Some even glared, though it was not for long before they became distracted by the sight of Lawrence. For his part, he did his best to keep pace with her; for a small girl, she walked fast, apparently not caring whether he walked next to or behind her.

It was not until they had left the town center behind, and were instead making their way down narrow, winding streets, that Josephine slowed her step.

"Henry spoke about you sometimes," she said. "Sorry, I mean Doctor Berkeley."

"He was Henry to me as well," he said, gently. "I suspect he told you to call him that."

"Yeah. Like you did, with your name."

"And what did Henry say of me, then?"

"That you were at university together. That you were his friend and if anything happened I should contact you. Didn't have your address though, or I couldn't remember it."

"May I ask—were you one of his patients? The letter I received mentioned an illness in town."

"No, I wasn't sick. Not a lot of people were, but all those that were have died."

"Was your—I am sorry to ask, but you mentioned that your father had died…"

"That was something else." She looked away, her throat bopping. He allowed her a moment to compose herself. "That was…he got a nail stuck in his leg, real deep. We were living somewhere else. Doctor treated it and got it out, but then later the rot set in." She swallowed again. "They cut the leg off, and he was better for a while, but then suddenly he was sick again. They tried to cut off more, but…I guess it was too late."

"And when…when was this?"

They had started walking slower and slower. "Two years ago."

"My condolences, Josephine."

"Don't need them, won't bring him back," she said, rather brusquely, and Lawrence stopped in shock. Whatever anger was on her face melted away again. "Sorry. I know you mean well, I just got sick of hearing that. People would say it to me, but it was people who had always underpaid him or even refused to buy from him, just because…"

She stopped abruptly, pink rising to her cheeks. "Nevermind. Don't know why I'm talking so much."

Lawrence rather thought it was because she finally had a listening audience. He knew what that was like—knew how intoxicating it could be, the reason why he had foolishly spilled his secrets to Henry, and before that to…

"I suppose it was because he was black, yes?"

Her eyes flashed. "How'd you know?"

"An educated guess."

Josephine huffed, but her body angled slightly towards him, her arms crossed over her chest. "Yeah. Yeah. Most people can't tell, I guess my ma must have been light-skinned and I take after her. Explains this." She tugged at her braid of thick red curls.

Lawrence's tongue felt too heavy in his mouth. "You did not know her?"

"No, and pa would never tell me anything. Said I just didn't have a mom, only a father and wasn't he enough?" She started walking again, staring right ahead. "He was enough. Until he was gone."

Lawrence trailed after her. He did his level best to ignore the sound of tears she was desperately trying to hide from him, though he ached to say something. He blamed the tears in his own eyes on the wind.

VI.

ENRY'S GRAVE WAS unassuming, his name and two dates the only features on the stone. Whoever had engraved them had done so with care, at least. Lawrence was glad for that.

Now that he was here, Lawrence realized he had not known what to expect. A sign that this was all some cosmic joke, perhaps? His friend, hale and alive, and laughing at the bewilderment on his face? But no, Henry had never been one for pranks, especially not cruel ones. Perhaps he had thought that Josephine would show him to a grave saying *Henry Blarkley* or *Henry Berkerly* or *Henry Morgan, terror of the seas,* and he could have pointed at the name and said, *no, look, that was not my dear friend's name, you must have had him mixed up with someone else! This has all been a misunderstanding.*

The smell of rotten fish drifted in from the harbor. No matter where one walked in this town, it seemed the smells and sounds of the sea found you. His lungs burned, staring at the gravestone. Here laid Henry, one of the finest men he had ever known; dead and gone forever. And moments ago, he had learned of the death of another fine man, one he had parted ways with before either of them were ready. One he might have been able to save from his fate, had he only stayed by his side.

It was all too much; he wished to weep, but he was far too tired. What had Henry called it? The inevitability of a lack of omnipotence. He had been the one to drag Lawrence away from the sickbeds, the infirmaries, the hospitals, and say *sleep, you are dead on your feet, you will not help them by falling over and braining yourself on the floor.*

But Lawrence had always been stubborn. He had always wanted to do more, do better—to treat not only the symptoms, but to find the very root of the disease. To learn. To *know.*

"Josephine," he said, eyes boring holes into the earth as if he could see beyond the grave. "Do you know where I might acquire a shovel?"

THEY WAITED, RATHER sensibly, until night had fallen again. Lawrence found himself pacing in his room, once more unable to sleep. Exhaustion was starting to creep in at the edges of his vision, but there was too much nervous energy running through his body for him to lie down now.

After their walk to the cemetery and subsequent planning, Lawrence had spent the rest of the day visiting Henry's patients in town. It seemed the ones who had suffered from whatever illness had run through town truly were dead, as Josephine had said; the family who remained, those who'd had brushes with the ill, been checked over, treated for other things. Most of said things were old age and pain in the joints, or failing limbs from years and years of hard work. Lawrence did not mind checking them over. What he did mind was the way they all *stared* at him. It was not wholly uncomfortable, though some clearly seemed reluctant to even let him inside their homes. He did not mind;

Lawrence was used to patients who mistrusted doctors on principle, especially those who came from the big city. He only tried his best to put them at ease. Not that most of them were actually sick—one man in particular made a show of coughing, but Lawrence could tell, after years of working with hypochondriacs and lazy bastards wanting a day off work, that the coughing was faked. He still smiled and told the man to take it easy for a few days.

What he *did* mind were the other kind of stares. The ones that seemed assessing, like Richards' had been, combing over every bit of him as if they could peel apart his secrets, one by one. Lawrence hated that—had been subjected to those kinds of looks before, and it had rarely ended well. For anyone.

He still smiled and bore it, as he always did. What struck him the most was that it was the same look—the same, always the same. From the townsfolk and Richards, even from Marlyn and Thompson. The same.

Still, there were some who were kind. A couple of youngsters had come up and given him a bunch of flowers—weeds, truly, more than anything—and asked him a few questions. Then there was young Mrs. Sinclair, bereft of her husband but with her belly near bursting with child. She had smiled at him, but it had been so tired; he was rather worried she would not live long after the child was born, from exhaustion if nothing else.

Those patients had all been glad to have Henry there, sharing that the doctor had helped them with their ailments, had made their parents feel better, had even saved a man when he had almost drowned. They were sad that he was gone. They were glad to have a new doctor in town.

Lawrence did not have the heart to tell them that he was not staying. It wouldn't have been entirely true, anyway. He didn't *plan* to stay, but he had meant to be gone by now, long before night could fall on Osmund once more.

Josephine had changed that. Even with this burning urge to find out what had really happened to Henry, he would have been hard-pressed to stay had it not been for her. It might have been different had her father still been around, but he knew now that she was alone. He could not leave her. He had a sickening feeling that Richards' knew, but if he knew then…

Then perhaps Henry had gotten drunk after all. Had been telling secrets he had once sworn to keep.

The thought left an acrid taste in the back of his throat, and he tried his best to push it away. He did not know, and he did not wish to condemn his friend without any evidence.

Finally, Josephine came to fetch him from his room, but he stumbled in shock when he saw that she was not alone.

"Hello," Marlyn said.

"Oh, hello."

Josephine looked at him, rather defiant. "Marlyn had the shovel. And he's sneaky. Like I said."

The youth gave him a tremulous smile, his eyes darting back and forth between them. Lawrence bit the inside of his cheek.

"And young Marlyn can keep a secret?"

It took Marlyn a moment to register that the question was directed at him. "Uhm, uh, oh, yes, um sir. Doctor. Doctor, sir."

Lawrence did not believe him for a moment, but Josephine looked confident. Despite his misgivings, he wished to trust her; in fact, he found it suddenly imperative that she should know he believed in her. Damn it all; damn Henry and damn the Reverend. It all came back to Josephine, and now he was trapped here.

They did their best to be stealthy as they ventured outside the inn and began the trek back towards the cemetery. Everything around them was silent, save for the lapping of the waves—and Lawrence's pounding heart, booming like a cannon in his ears.

All too soon they were at the grave. They took turns with the shovel, having only the one, while the others kept a watch; soon it was Josephine and Marlyn digging, as they found Lawrence's technique and speed quite lacking. It was left to him to stand with one of the lanterns, gazing out into the dark around them. He was aware that he was not a very good watchman—his heart was still going far too loud, and the scrape of the shovel digging into the earth seemed to be all he could focus on. Even his eyes failed him; it seemed the shadows moved, taking humanoid shapes one moment, fading back into hills of grass or harmless trees the next.

Then came a *thunk* as the shovel hit something solid; Lawrence startled, nearly dropping the lantern. Marlyn kept digging with a grim set to his mouth.

Finally the coffin was unearthed. Lawrence jumped down to aid in wrenching the lid loose, but Josephine was already making short work of it. She spirited a hammer from somewhere, banging and dragging until the nails came out; they landed in the dirt at her feet, twisted and discarded. Marlyn had to climb back out of the grave to make room for Lawrence to join her down there. He stood above, shovel still in his hands, and Lawrence had the unpleasant thought that it would be easy for the other man to hit them both over the head and bury them down there. Discard any evidence that he had been part of this crime.

Josephine opened the lid, and the stench hit them. Lawrence was not unused to the smell of decay; he had vomited the first time he had attended a public autopsy, but Henry had *fainted,* so he had not felt too bad about it. After that, it had become easier, though it had been a year before the dizzy spells had stopped whenever he had to cut into dead flesh. Lawrence had never gotten used to it in the clinical way the morticians sometimes had about them (he hoped he never would), but it became easier every time he did it.

This was something else. He'd known, of course, that it would be different, unearthing the already-decaying corpse of his dearest friend, but he had not been prepared for the smell of rotting fish to hit him, had not been prepared to look into the coffin, coated in slime and briny water, the smell of dead flesh mingling with the tangy smells of the earth and ocean both.

Lawrence almost vomited, as he had when he'd been a green youth. Josephine gasped, then promptly clapped a hand over her mouth and nose to keep from breathing in too deep. They both stared down the coffin, at the corpse of Doctor Henry Berkeley.

He had now the bloated face of a corpse adrift in the sea for days upon days. His skin was blue, his hair a dark and slimy mess; it still clung to the skin, but the skin did not cling to the bone. It seemed to be sloughing off, and when the fresh air and the light of the moon hit it, the whole face shifted, half a cave-in, half a glide to the side.

Above them, he thought he heard Marlyn retch. Lawrence fumbled to take out a handkerchief, bringing it up to cover his nose and mouth. On the other side of the coffin, he could hear Josephine's panicked breaths, muffled by her hands.

Lawrence could not rely on a deep breath to steady himself, so he instead counted slowly to ten in his head; when he was done, he leaned down closer, bringing the lantern with him. His eyes stung from the odor, but he would not be deterred. Not when he had come so far.

Henry's clothes were coarse, a simple shirt that had almost merged with his chest. Yet, he was still recognizable, and Lawrence realized he had hoped that they might open the coffin and find a decoy, a different corpse, one he could definitively say was not his friend. But no; in spite of the horrid decay of the flesh, the dead man looked like Henry.

Lawrence felt dizzy again, and he thought he should rather get up, get out of here. The longer he stared at the corpse, the worse he felt. *Of course,* he thought. *What were you thinking, man? You've desecrated the final resting place of your one and only friend. What are you* doing?

He must have lost his mind. He stood up, ready to scramble out of the grave, when Josephine spoke:

"What's that? Around his neck?"

Before he could respond, she had reached forward, fingers glancing over a thin chain. When they touched the skin of the corpse's neck, pieces of it seemed to stick to her fingertips, and she quickly pulled her hand away with a sound of disgust.

But the movement had pulled at the chain too, pulling the necklace free from the shirt and into view. Lying above Henry's heart was a small medallion, round and pale silver. It was untouched by the rot surrounding it; engraved on it was a slim tree, branches curling both upwards and down. Lawrence reached down with the handkerchief, grasping the medallion gently and, almost without coherent thought, pulled at it.

The chain sliced through the neck cleanly, as if it was butter, coming free and letting the head roll to the side, a horrid mockery of a man turning in bed to sleep better.

"Oh, *fuck,*" Josephine muttered, and Lawrence did not have the heart to scold her for her language right that minute. He quickly wrapped the medallion up and put it in his pocket, before climbing out of the grave.

"Are we done? Can we be done?" Marlyn asked. The man looked terribly pale under the moonlight, a sheen of sweat covering his face.

"Yes, yes, we're done," Lawrence assured him. He turned to help Josephine out of the grave, her fingers only minutely trembling against his palm; in fact, it might be he who was trembling. "Let's… let's fill it up again."

They worked in silence, Lawrence doing most of the work this time. It seemed Josephine had reached her threshold for this insane adventure. She sat down to take the watch, lantern beside her, knees tugged up to her chest. She stared right ahead, not once looking back at them as Marlyn trembled and Lawrence poured dirt back over the coffin. The smell did not leave his nose; at this point he feared it never would.

When they had finished, Marlyn covered the grave in handfuls of reedy flowers and grass, to make it less apparent what they had done. Lawrence felt sick, looking at it: people would believe the flowers had been left by Henry's dear old friend, come to visit. No one would suspect that he had done something so heinous, had even dragged two young, innocent people into it…

"We speak of this to no-one, understand?" he said, as the three of them stood shoulder to shoulder, staring at the grave. "Not even each other. It will be as if this never happened."

They agreed in quiet whispers, and then Marlyn led them to a quiet stretch of beach, where they could wash off the worst of the dirt and muck. Even here it smelled horrid, but the stench of the ocean was far preferable to the grave, and the breeze was fresh, if harsh. Lawrence took a deep breath.

The salt of the ocean-water stung his hands as he plunged them in, but even that felt like a relief. His arms and shoulders ached, though he would not complain of it while his young companions were silent on their own miseries. They washed up. Lawrence, almost on a whim, brought out the medallion, letting it stay in the handkerchief as he soaked it, before unwrapping the sodden thing.

The water seemed to clean away the slime easily, and the necklace was as new, shining brightly under the stars. It was a beautiful, if simple piece, but Lawrence had not the faintest idea where Henry might have gotten it.

Or why—the man had never been much for jewelry, especially once Lawrence had shown him how much dirt could accumulate in rings and between the small links of a chain.

He suddenly missed Henry with a fierce ache, something he hadn't felt since the last time he'd seen… Henry had understood him, had listened to his rants about cleanliness and how important it was, *especially* for a surgeon. What did it matter if you operated, if infection set in nine times out of ten, simply because there was still old blood on your hands? When a simple scrub with soap and water could *save lives*.

He glanced at Josephine, sure that she would understand if he told her, but for now the girl was simply staring into the water, her brow furrowed. What she'd seen tonight would mark her, he knew, and he ached with regrets both old and new.

He made his decision, however fear-inducing it might be. "Josephine," he said, waiting patiently for her to look at him. "Are you alright?"

She took her time to answer, which he appreciated. "Yeah," she said. "I don't know. I think."

"I am sorry for making you go through that. I should not have involved you."

She looked away, jaw set. "I wanted to be here."

We always think we know what we want, Lawrence heard, as if from far away, in an old friend's voice. *It never shapes out like we envisioned.*

He took a moment to think on what he wanted to say next. "Josephine, I am…leaving, tomorrow."

By the sharp look she gave him, she had both been expecting and dreading that. He took it as a good sign.

"Well, you've seen what you wanted to see, I expect."

"No. Or, rather, yes. But, and forgive me for being tactless in pointing this out, but I have rather noticed that you do not seem happy here. Do you have no other family you could go to, elsewhere in the country?"

By her wide eyes, she hadn't expected that question. "No," she said, slowly. "It was just me and my pa. Now it's just me."

Yes, he had rather feared that. "I was wondering, then, if you would like a better position than your work at the inn? I confess, I do not know what you make of money, but as it happens, my landlady is in need of an assistant and she would pay handsomely—not to mention, she needs someone who is not me to dote on." He said the last bit with an awkward chuckle that did nothing to relieve the sudden tension.

Long moments of dreadful silence passed, before she finally spoke. "What is this? Why are you…"

"It is nothing untoward," he assured her. "Ah, I realize you barely know me. And that I rather just involved you in some criminal activity. In fact, you would be rather mad to listen to me at all."

But she was not shouting or hurling accusations, or storming away. She was still looking at him, both of them crouched by the water, waves coming up to kiss their shoes.

"You have no reason to trust me, but I assure you this is not some nebulous scheme to…to, I don't know. Rather a lot of work for that, isn't it? I assure you, if you trusted Henry, then you can trust me. And you may even…give it some thought. I could come back for you if you say no and later change your mind." He would hate to come back here once he was free of the place, but for Josephine he would do it.

"I do though, is the thing," she said. "I do trust you. I don't know why, but you just…" She looked away again. "I don't know if I should. I just do."

"Well, if it is any consolation, I once told dear Henry my greatest secret on a whim." *A rather drunken whim, that is.* "We only became greater friends after that."

"And what secret is that?"

His heart pounded, heavy with fear again. He forced himself to smile. "I will tell you, one day." When he had gained the impossible courage to do so.

"That a promise?"

She looked so much like her father then, sitting in the moonlight, daring him to lie to her. *Do you promise me?*

"Yes, Josephine. One day I will tell you."

It was not until they got up again, shaking water from their hands, that he noticed Marlyn had already left.

L AWRENCE FINALLY SLEPT—PERHAPS it was the decision to leave that calmed him enough to do so. The finality of it, knowing that he would soon be back in the city, back in his own home, with Mrs. Danson and her tea. And hopefully with Josephine there—she had not given him a final answer, but by the look in her eyes, he thought himself well-placed to hope for a yes.

That was not to say that he slept easy. In his dreams, he was swimming in the vast ocean, dark as midnight; not a moon or star in sight. Ahead of him, bopping on the waves, was Henry, face turned upwards, maggots crawling from his mouth, his nose. He was moaning, saying something, a repeat of things he had told Lawrence before; things Lawrence had been too preoccupied to take notice of. *I am sorry,* he wanted to say, but his mouth filled with brackish water. It was not the sea, he thought; it was too heavy for the sea. It filled him to the brink.

There had been no maggots in the coffin, he realized, as he sunk down deeper. Nothing had wished to gnaw on that flesh. Henry had been, by all sense of the word, *dead*, when in fact most corpses were living organisms, a teeming colony of beings feasting, thriving on what had once been a person. But not in this place.

A better man would stay to figure out the mystery, to bring peace to his dead friend. But Lawrence had never claimed to be brave—no matter what others had told him. No, staying here was senseless. He would go with Josephine, he would contact Henry's family, have them sort it out. With their money and influence, it would not be a problem for them to have the body returned, to find out if something nefarious had happened. It was not his responsibility. He did not know why the Reverend had even contacted him in the first place.

Lawrence sank deeper. He had almost reached the bottom of the sea, when he woke up.

IT WAS MARLYN who woke him. It only occurred to Lawrence much later to ask him how he had gotten in, since he knew he had locked the door—he *always* did, no matter where he was. But for now he was distracted by the sight of the man over him.

"Doctor…"

"Good Lord, man, what happened to your eye?!"

Marlyn blinked; or at least half of a blink, since his left eye was too swollen to do so, already turning black and blue. "Got into a fight," he mumbled. "One of the men at the docks."

When had he even had time to do that? Lawrence couldn't have been sleeping for more than four hours, though dawn was coming quick.

"What…"

"It's Mrs. Sinclair," Marlyn said, and it took a few moments for Lawrence's brain to even remember who that was. "She's giving birth, sir."

Lawrence was on his feet in an instant, grabbing his bag and throwing his coat on; he almost tripped in his haste, but this was not the first time he had been woken in the middle of the night because a patient was going into labor. He knew what to do.

Mrs. Sinclair—Marie, he reminded himself, her first name was Marie—was in a great deal of pain by the time he got there. Another woman was with her, speaking gently and holding her hand—she blanched when Lawrence arrived, as if not having expected him to be there. He had checked her son for the fever, he recalled, only the day before. Her eyes had been assessing too—and judgmental.

"Right, then," he said, smiling brightly, ignoring the clench in his throat. "Let's get this show going, shall we?"

The whole affair ended bloody. Lawrence saw from the beginning the fear in Marie's wide eyes, and he knew that something was wrong. A quick calculation, based on what she had told him, proved that she was early. Much too early.

Lawrence had dealt with this before. He had been a doctor for years now, and this was not the first complication he had met during childbirth. It was quite easy, now, to shed his misgivings, his fear and exhaustion, and instead focus on the work at hand so intently that the rest of the world faded away. People came and left; they fetched what he asked for, listened to his orders. They held dear Marie's hand as she pushed and screamed. Lawrence barely noticed them, save for the use they had in this. Marie was more important—the babe was more important. He had to focus.

A cut was necessary. Lawrence had done so before, but always he needed to take a moment to steel himself. A bloody affair.

When Lawrence finally held the child in his arms, he almost dropped it. It was not a…it was just that as he held it…looking at it in the faint glow of the candlelight inside Marie's tiny hut of a house…it was just that the child was…

Barely a child at all. It resembled, more than anything, a strange fish-like creature, gills etched into the sides of the neck, skin a sickly, pale green. Even that he could have understood—infants fresh from the womb, especially those cut out and born too early, were often strange-looking. But what scared him this time was that it resembled, more than anything, the corpse of Henry. The same pallor. The same hollow eyes, the same skin that seemed to cling to his hands and *slough* off.

The babe let out one, shrill cry and then fell silent again. Marie had passed out, but even in her comatose state, she was crying. Lawrence could barely breathe, and when he did find it in himself to do so, the air felt sticky in his lungs, heavy as molasses, dry as dust.

He placed the newborn child on Marie's chest, hands trembling. He went to wash his hands, finding the water in the basin coarse; pulled from the sea. It was half the mother's blood, half his own, he realized; he must have cut himself on his scalpel or something of the like.

Somehow, Reverend Richards was there. "Here, doctor," he said. "Come along back now. Your work here is done, you need to rest."

By the time Lawrence woke up, back at the inn, the entire day had passed him by and night had fallen once more. He'd stayed in Osmund another day.

HE SLEPT THROUGH the entire night as well, waking only to drink from the water placed by his bedside. It tasted foul, but he was thirsty enough to not care. Only the next morning, when he woke lightheaded and with a river of nausea in his stomach, did he realize it tasted like the hot drink he'd been served that first night.

He went to empty his stomach, but could only retch up empty air. There was a knock on the door, and he called for more time. The door-handle rattled, but it was locked. Thankfully.

Lawrence felt wretched when he went to open the door, but it was only Josephine on the other side. Her eyes were hooded, bloodshot. She appeared to have not slept in a while.

"You're to…the…Marie's son is dead. Could you go to her, please?"

There was not much to do for her, truth be told. Marie already held the quiet, calm acceptance of someone who had expected this to happen long ago. The remains had already been taken away.

Lawrence stayed by her, checked the stitches, had her drink more water and decreed that she be served only soup and light foods for the next month.

"I am very sorry," he told her, when the quiet had gotten to him. "For your loss. I have no platitudes to give you, only a doctor's care. If there is anything I can do…"

She interrupted him: "Have you ever had children, doctor?"

His mouth tasted like ash. "No. I haven't."

Marie stared past him. "Nor have I."

He did not know what to make of that. He almost asked, but then the shadows moved, and a figure, large and foreboding appeared. Lawrence almost shrieked, but then the scant light from the windows fell on Thompson's face.

The man stared at him. Even in the heat of Marie's room, he wore his heavy coat. It trailed onto the floor, covering every part of him. He walked as if his left side pained him, limping—slightly hunched.

He said nothing; only stared at Lawrence, as if expecting him to understand. Marie gently reached for his hand, squeezing his fingers.

"It is time for you to go," she said. Lawrence hurried outside; Thompson stayed behind.

HE FOUND HIS way to the church. It was on a whim more than anything; the building was foreboding in the dimness of the day here. The church was old as the town though it stood a little apart from it, closer to the sea; perhaps it was even older than the rest of Osmund. It seemed to live in that unknowable existence between ready to fall over at any moment, and so ancient it might stand forever. A few windows were broken, boarded up; the others shone light through the stained glass, a picture of some blue-eyed saint he did not recognize gazing out at him.

Inside, the careful cleaning of the stone tiles could not hide the wear and tear. Skeletons were etched among the pews and onto the stone-floors, and the chandeliers seemed to hoard all the warmth, leaving the rest of the hall cold as winter. The scattered windows that were not boarded up were dusty enough to keep the faint sunlight out.

Reverend Richards was sorting crates by the altar. He looked up as Lawrence approached, smiling at him in that genial way he had. It fell away when he saw the expression on Lawrence's face.

"I heard about poor Mrs. Sinclair," Richards said. "We have the child here, presently. He was not baptized, so we cannot bury him on holy ground, but he will receive a burial nonetheless. Such a shame, but unfortunately not an uncommon occurrence in these parts."

Lawrence looked at the crates, a morbid part of him expecting to find remains in there. It was wine, stacked. Cheap altar-wine, in dusty bottles, he guessed.

"Have you any theories as to why? I have handled plenty of births, but none of the children looked so…" *Ghoulish.* That was it. A ghoul. Lawrence had held children born with their legs fused—small merfolk, as the uneducated called them, and he had even seen newborns with aberrations on their flesh that might look like gills or other animal-like attributes. But this had been different.

"Some of the townsfolk say the town is cursed," Richards said. "But I do not believe that. God is too good to curse a town for no reason. The people here have done nothing wrong; they are simply living their lives." He sighed. "Perhaps it is something in the water. The grog we brew here is stronger than anything I have ever tried before."

Lawrence believed that. "Do you still have Henry's belongings? Perhaps he made some notes that could be useful."

"But of course! They are back at the inn. I will find them for you tonight." He reached out, clasped Lawrence's shoulder. It was gentle, but Lawrence had not welcomed touch in a long time, not since he had last been in love. He took a short step to the side. Reverend Richards did not seem to notice the dismissal. "It is so very good to have you here with us, doctor."

"I do not plan to stay long," he said, because he needed to say it out loud, especially to the Reverend who had brought him here in the first place.

"Oh, I know. Josephine mentioned you have spoken of taking her with you. That is good—a clever girl like that should have more opportunities."

Lawrence forced a smile, and made to step away, only to find Richards had taken hold of his arm again.

"Here," he said. "Here, take this, as a thanks for all that you have already done. Oh, I see your face—it is not thin wine for the church, but a vintage from the vineyard we own in the South. These crates have stood in reserve for a while, but I thought it time to break them out."

The bottle was a deep green, the label painted in flaking yellow. Lawrence was not sure how he managed to hold one without dropping it, letting it shatter on the church-floor. In simple details, the label had a sketch of a spindly tree, branches swooping both upwards and down.

LAWRENCE KNEW BETTER. He truly did. Yet he still found himself opening the bottle of wine, alone in his room, pouring the deep-red liquid into a tin cup, scrubbed clean with harsh hands. The wine looked and smelled fine enough. He ended up putting the cup down on the floor next to him, not drinking at all.

What am I doing?

He had lost sight of it all. He was exhausted to his very bones, and it had been days now, when he never should have come here at all. Not alone, at least. Not even for Henry.

It had been a dream of theirs—to travel, parting ways because the smaller towns usually only had room for one doctor, but converging, finding each other again. It was Lawrence who had grown complacent—Lawrence who had seen the name of the first destination Henry had planned for, and blanched.

I thought you said you had been there before, Henry had said
I have, yes. That was rather the problem.

He supposed he could ask Josephine when she and her
father had moved away from that place, how long they had
lived in Osmund—and thereby know if his concerns back
then had even been warranted. Perhaps he would not have
run into her and her father, not at any point. There were only
so many places he could be. And even if they had run into
each other, would it have been such a bad thing? Lawrence
had made the choice, but that had been years ago. There was
no reason they could not be cordial to each other, as distant
strangers who had once been friends. Fear had kept him
back, as it so often did. And now it had cost Henry his life.

No more of this. Lawrence was no detective, but he
intended to get to the bottom of it. He carefully rose and
put the cup and bottle on the desk. Where to start? These
strange happenings had been Henry's thing, always
fascinated with mysteries of any nature. Lawrence only
liked the mysteries he saw behind glass or beneath his
scalpel. Still, he had to try. For Henry. He began his
search.

He found nothing in the room, save dust beneath the
bed and a marked page in the Shakespeare collection,
denoting the start of a particular Scottish play. He needed
Henry's things, his journal. They would hold some clue,
he was sure of it.

Feeling invigorated, if fearful, he walked downstairs.
The inn was empty of people, though it was still early
evening. Reverend Richards was still at work in the
church, he supposed. He should have insisted he fetch the
things immediately. If he even wanted to relinquish them.

The lanterns fluttered—the inn was cold, the fireplace
unlit. He shivered. A hand rested on his shoulder. He
screamed and whirled around.

Josephine screamed too, and jumped back, away from
him. "What the…"

"Oh, Josephine! I am so sorry, my dear, you quite startled me!"

"What the *fuck*, I was just walking up to you…"

"Language!"

"Yeah, yeah, sorry…I didn't mean…" It was difficult to tell against her skin, and in the dim light, but he thought she was blushing. He almost laughed. John had gotten loud when embarrassed too, always swearing up a storm.

John.

The name hit him like a punch to the gut. He had not let himself even think it, not in over a decade. But suddenly, he knew what to do.

"Josephine, would you sit with me a moment? Just here."

"Yes. I meant to ask if you wanted dinner, I can…"

"No, no, that's quite fine. Please, sit."

She did so, across from him this time. The benches really were uncomfortable, but Lawrence refrained from grimacing as he sat down. Josephine was watching him carefully.

"I have a confession to make to you," he told her.

She said nothing, only watched him. She hid it well, but Lawrence could tell he was frightening her. Best get it over with—but of course, now his tongue was stumbling, refusing to even walk when he needed it to run. It was raining again, outside. It seemed to always rain in this blasted town, and if not rain then it was the morning-fog, and if not that then hail or heavy clouds promising to open up the floodgates at any moment.

"I knew your father," he finally said. "A long time ago, I knew him. We were friends."

What a simple word to describe all they had been to each other. But it was not untrue.

Josephine frowned. "Oh. He never mentioned you."

He had known that—had wanted that, even, but hearing it still sent a pang of hurt through his chest. "No, he would not have. This was before…right before you were born. He and I had a…I will not say a falling out, we parted on amicable enough terms. But we had a difference of…opinion, and thought it best to go our separate ways."

She was watching him so carefully now, eyes dark and glinting. He recalled Henry saying it of him once, *you watch me like I am some interesting bug, sometimes.* This must be what that felt like.

"Was it because of my mother?"

"I beg your pardon?" His voice went high-pitched, hands clenching in shock.

"Why you and my pa weren't friends anymore—were you both in love with my mother or something?"

"What…no, no, nothing of the sort." He laughed, a little hysterically. "I never even knew her." *And nor did he.*

"Why didn't you tell me before?"

It was a fair question. "I suppose I was scared," he said. "And I was shocked when you said that he was…dead."

Something like understanding dawned on her face. "Did you love him?"

It was not in Lawrence's to lie any longer. Not about this. "Yes," he said. "I did. Rather much so."

"As a brother?"

He almost agreed, because that was the easy answer, but the look Josephine was giving him…just as John had, once upon a time, she had already figured out the truth of the matter, and was only looking for confirmation. He would not break her trust by lying to her so openly now.

"No, no. Not as a brother."

It had been everything, at the time. They had both been so young, both so convinced that society's rules did not apply to them, not if they simply tried hard enough. John had discovered his secret by accident, but it had changed nothing save to push them even closer together. The two of them, who should not have been as much as friends—pale, short Lawrence, about to go to university, and dark, tall John, the son of a carpenter, never expected to rise above his station. Even them breathing too long in the same space was scandalous, let alone keep up a friendship. Let alone…

"Oh," Josephine said. "Reverend Richards said love between two men is a sign of the Devil."

There was no condemnation in her voice; only a question.

Lawrence took a deep breath. "It is not. It is…" He hesitated.

"It is?" Her voice was gentle as she prompted him.

Lawrence wasn't sure exactly. "Not that."

Josephine accepted with a nod. She rose from the table, a little abruptly. "I'll go make us some dinner."

And just like that, it was done with. Lawrence almost laughed with relief, though he thought he might instead crying if he did. Her footsteps were light; he gently rested his head in his hands, breathing deep.

His solace was interrupted when there was a commotion from the kitchen. *"Marlyn!"* he heard Josephine yell, as he jumped up to assist. *"What* are you doing back here?!"

She did not sound in danger, only exasperated. He could not hear Marlyn's reply, only the soft, stammered cadence of his voice. He sat back down, letting the voices wash over him. Breathing a sigh of relief.

L AWRENCE WENT TO the church again the next day, intent on finding the Reverend and asking for Henry's journal directly.

He was surprised to find that Richards already had company. Marlyn stood with him by the altar, both of them looking towards the door as it opened. Marlyn did not seem pleased to see him, and looked away. Reverend Richards smiled, as always.

"Ah, Reverend, I was hoping to speak with you in private," he said, feeling suddenly very embarrassed, yet suspicious of what he had stumbled upon. "But it can wait, if you are busy."

"No, no, not at all." Lawrence clasped Marlyn's shoulder, fingers digging into the thin shirt. "We were just finishing up, weren't we?"

Marlyn nodded, still looking away. Lawrence felt a chill run down his spine—had Marlyn told the Reverend what they had done? Had he heard something from the kitchen yesterday? He was ashamed to admit that he had not even considered the thought, so giddy had he been that Josephine had not cast him out after the reveal.

"If you're sure," Lawrence said, but Marlyn was already stammering out a goodbye and scurrying towards the door. It fell closed with a loud echo, cascading through the wide halls of the church. Lawrence stared after him.

"Do not be concerned," said Richards, as if reading his mind. "Marlyn is merely worried about Josephine leaving. He is quite fond of her, you see."

"Indeed." Lawrence frowned. "She is a bit young for him, though." Even as he said it, he knew it was not uncommon, especially in these parts. And Marlyn was still young—it was only that, for all his apparent insecurities, Marlyn was an adult and Josephine was fifteen. Lawrence's own family had not started speaking of marriage until he was nineteen.

"It is nothing of that sort, don't you worry. In fact, Marlyn has always been quite uninterested in matters of the heart. I suspect it is more that redheads must stick together, yes?" Richards laughed. Lawrence felt compelled to smile, though he did not feel like it, and Richards seemed to sense that he did not find it funny. He said: "He had a little sister, once."

"Marlyn did?"

"Yes. She died in quite a horrible way. On the very steps of this church, in fact. Murdered by her own father."

"That is terrible!" Lawrence's voice rang through the church, and he flinched at the sound of it.

"Indeed. The folk here say the ocean had driven him insane. He was at sea fishing more than he was ever at home.

Her name was Katherine. Marlyn called her Kya."

A cart drove by outside; someone shouted. The response was not quite a laugh, but a ragged, broken sound that might have been laughter's cousin.

"What happened to the parents? Marlyn's and Kya's?"

"The mother drowned herself. The father was killed by a mob in town. Dreadful business."

Dreadful. Lawrence agreed. Everything about this town was dreadful.

"And what do you, as a priest, do when something like this happens in your town?"

Richards seemed surprised by the question. He took his time to answer.

"I speak with the people affected," he said. "And I pray, fervently, for something like this to never happen again." He was still smiling. "We are all Children of God, even the worst of us. We must hope for salvation in the next life, even as the sinners must be punished first."

"What kind of punishment would you mete out?"

"Oh, punishment is the purvey of God, not me."

"Truly. It seems the townsfolk here thought differently."

Richards hung his head. "One man cannot stop a raging mob, much as he might try. I am only trying to make the town better now, and move past the tragedies."

"It seems you have not succeeded," Lawrence said, before he could stop himself. Richards looked up at him, startled—it occurred to Lawrence that this was the first real, unfiltered emotion he had gotten from the other man. "My apologies," he said. "I did not mean…"

"No, you are quite right," Richard's said; he was smiling, again, as he composed himself. "Mysterious deaths, illness rampant, children born strange…with your expertise, when you cut free the child, I thought perhaps that would do it. We would finally have a success. A caesarean delivery is what they call it, no?"

"You are quite knowledgeable about medical procedures, Reverend."

"I am not a man of science, but I have looked up what I could. Before dear Berkeley came here, we were bereft of a proper medical man. And I must admit, I am quite the fan of Shakespeare."

"Shakespeare?"

"Yes. *Macbeth,* in particular. Macduff can kill the eponymous character only because he was cut from his mother's womb. You have not read the play, sir?"

"I have, but it has been a while."

The wind shuttered in through the broken windows, wrestling with the boards. "Yes, well, Macbeth is told by the witches that 'none of woman born shall harm Macbeth.' He thinks himself quite safe, but Macduff, as it turns out, was not born in the traditional manner, not at all." His eyes shone as he talked.

"Yes, I recall that now." Lawrence had not suspected the Reverend to be such a man of literature.

"It takes an extraordinary person to do extraordinary things. Such as fulfilling prophecy, or bringing about a proper change."

"It seems to me it should be one's actions, rather than the manner of one's birth that dictates what one does with their life." Again, he thought of John; cleverer and far kinder than most of the academic men Lawrence had met. If only he had been born in a different world, one where the color of his skin did not matter.

"We all have our destinies," the Reverend said.

"Quite. I am sorry to cut this conversation short." He definitely wasn't. "But I came here to ask for Henry's things? His journal in particular."

"Oh, of course! Forgive me, doctor, I completely forgot about it yesterday. After the hubbub of the birth, we all found ourselves quite busy and distraught. Give me just a moment."

He walked through a door behind the presbytery, one Lawrence had not even noticed before now. Mere seconds passed as he stood alone by the altar before he started feeling nervous. He shifted from foot to foot, looking down.

He was standing right on one of the stones with a carving of a skeleton. It was on its side, a cup upheld in one hand, as if in offering. Lawrence shifted away, careful that his feet would not touch any part of the carving. He found that he could not look away; the carving was simple, yet elegant, and it reminded him of the work on Henry's gravestone. The light shifting of his shoes against the stone made the barest whisper of a sound go through the church-hall. In here, he realized he could not hear the endless sounds of the ocean, so prevalent everywhere else in town. It was only him, and the wind.

The skeleton was wrong, he realized. The fingers around the stem of the up were elongated, too long, and from the curve of its spine jutted strange protrusions, small but unmistakable once he had noticed them. The teeth looked sharper, as if every one of them was a canine incisor. The barest of lights fell through the stained glass of the window, painting the single, staring eye-socket in gold—as if it was blinking out at him.

He stumbled back, hitting one of the pews and collapsing onto it. The wood groaned under his weight, as if the seat had not been used for eons. The light went out as a cloud passed by; the skeleton faded back into a normal carving.

"*Shit*," he muttered to himself, heart racing, and then cast a quick eye up in apology for swearing in the house of God. Lawrence was not a religious man, but it was better to be safe than sorry.

The door opened again, Reverend Richards appearing with a box in his arms. It occurred to Lawrence then that Richards had told him last night that the box was back at the inn.

"Here you are," Richards said, handing him the box. "His personal effects. I must admit, I could not find his suitcase last night, so I do not know where his clothes are. I will keep looking."

"Thank you, this is fine." He could see the journal, lying atop Henry's old pocket-watch and the cap he'd preferred for sunny weather. Lawrence could not imagine he had gotten much use out of it here. "May I also ask— Henry came here because of this illness that took out a good deal of the townspeople, yes?"

"That is correct."

"So it began before he got here. Do you, perhaps, have a record of who has died from it? Both before and after Henry's arrival."

Richards' eyes shone, as if Lawrence had just handed him a kingly gift.

"I do, indeed! We keep a record of every birth and every death in Osmund, have done so for the last two-hundred years. Wait here a moment."

Lawrence was once again left alone. He put the box down on the seat next to him, fingers gently touching the silk scarf, the cracked fountain pen, the pouch of tobacco. Henry had smoked very rarely, and indeed his pipe did not appear to be in the box at all. It was likely he had forgotten it somewhere and not bothered to get another.

He resolutely looked at nothing save for the box, afraid to meet the not-there eye of the skeleton again. The wind was still howling outside, and it had started to hail once more. Perhaps a heavy storm was coming; Lawrence certainly felt as if there was.

"Here you go." Reverend Richards came back carrying a heavy tome of a book. "This is for the last sixty years up until today. The illness started two years ago, though it only grew in number of infected in the last year or so. Please, take it with you."

"Are you sure? I can peruse it here." Lawrence

really did not wish to stay in the church for longer than necessary, but nicety won out over his misgivings.

"Oh, of course, take it. I trust you."

LAWRENCE FOUND HIMSELF back at the inn, reading under the candlelight. He had started with Henry's journal, eyes gliding over page after page until he finally came to when Henry had arrived in Osmund.

Nothing unusual appeared on the first few entries. Henry described the patients, who seemed to suffer from a bad bout of influenza more than anything else. The symptoms were severe, but such was not uncommon in towns with harsh environments and bad hygiene.

His hands started to tremble when he turned the page and saw Josephine mentioned. Henry's first notes were brief; he wrote that the girl had been a quick-witted assistant when he had needed to treat a man with an infection in the eyes. It was not until a page and a half later that he wrote about her again, remarking how easy the girl was to talk to, how she seemed to long for companionship of any kind: *she reminds me so much of…could there be an actual relation? I must introduce them to each other, one day.*

Lawrence almost slammed the book closed. Instead he leaned back against the wall—he had yet again found himself sitting on the cold, wooden floor rather than use the writing desk to read. He was not sure why, only that the low position on the floor afforded him a sense of safety. That, and like this he did not have to sit with his back to the door.

A sudden cramp shot through him, and he grimaced. Was that the date already? He endeavored to ignore it, for as long as he could. He had more important things to deal with right now.

He went back to reading, and in doing so realized that Henry must have stayed in this inn too. Of course! How had he not thought of that before? Perhaps whatever room he had occupied would hold some clue as to what had happened to him.

He quickly went downstairs, the journal tucked into his pocket. Richards stood behind the bar, cleaning glasses; he shot Lawrence a smile, but though he knew he could ask, he found he did not want Richards to know what he was looking for. Marlyn was there also, sitting at a table and nursing a beer. His eye had turned from blue and black to green and violet. Lawrence had offered to give him a cooling salve for it, but that had been met with a muttered *no, thank you.*

Josephine was in the kitchen. The door banged closed behind him.

"That's an entrance," Josephine said, while Lawrence grimaced. "Hello."

"Hello. I am sorry to disturb you, but I had a question. Where was Henry staying, while he was here?"

She put down the plate she had been cleaning. "Here at the inn? The room next to yours. He had yours at the start, but he said it was too drafty, the window couldn't close properly."

"Really?" Lawrence had had no such problem. "Could you show me the room?"

He was about to assure her it did not have to be right away, as she looked busy—and for a moment he had an image of the two of them, cleaning and drying off the dishes together. A very domestic scene, one he was sure John and she had done together, before his death. A proper family, doing menial chores, making them better with company.

But she was already drying her hands on her apron. "Of course. Let's go."

Marlyn had left by the time they got out of the kitchen, and Richards seemed preoccupied with putting glasses back on the shelf behind the bar. Lawrence tried to walk on tiptoes, but Josephine seemed to have no compunctions, walking confidently up the stairs as if she was not shirking her duties to help him sneak around.

When they arrived at the door to the left of Lawrence's room, she produced a ring of keys, easily finding the right one to fit in the lock. It swung open with a creak.

It was dark inside, and it smelled musty like a room unused for weeks, standing empty with the door closed. It held a rather large closet instead of a dresser, and the bed and writing-desk were both bigger than the ones he had at his disposal. A copy of *King Lear* rested there, alongside another Bible. Somewhere inside the room there was a faint scuttle, as if a rat or a mouse was creeping around in the shadows.

Lawrence went to fetch the candle from his own room, but when he got back he found Josephine had already walked inside. She had opened the door to the closet, but it looked entirely empty.

"Perhaps press on the back of it," he suggested. At the strange look she gave him, he went on: "There might be, ah, a hidden door or some such."

She looked skeptical, but she obliged, pressing her fingers against the wood. It creaked as she applied pressure, but nothing else happened. "There's nothing here."

Lawrence went over to try, keeping the candle in front of him, away from Josephine's wild curls and his own loose shirt. Even with a light to help, the closet showed nothing remarkable to the naked eye.

"Hmm."

"Do you still mean it?"

He blinked, coming out of his intense investigation. "Beg your pardon?"

Josephine would not meet his eyes. "I only mean…it's been days, now. I understand why you're staying, but…do you still mean that you'll take me with you? When you go?"

Yes, of course, he thought immediately, but he found he could not speak at all. He had failed to reassure her when the plan had changed, he saw that now. For all her maturity and cleverness, she was still a young girl and he had made her a promise and then seemingly ignored it, more occupied with anything else but her.

She seemed to misinterpret his look. "I'm not begging," she said, chin raised in defiance, even as he could see the soft hurt in her eyes. "That's not…only, if something had happened, it would only be right for you to tell me. If the plan had changed. If you'd spoken to someone else about it—*I* haven't mentioned it to anyone else," she added, as if that had been a concern of his.

"Of course I meant it, Josephine." Oh, but it felt strange to say her name—delightfully so. *This is all you gave up,* he thought, and felt a little hysterical. *Any chance to be a parent. Is it here, now? Is it here?*

"Nothing *of course* about it," she hissed. "People break their promises all the time. People leave, all the time."

He somehow found the courage within himself to rest a hand on her shoulder, light enough that she could step away from it if she wanted. She stayed put.

"I will not leave without you, Josephine," he swore to her. "I stayed because of you; because I saw you were… John's daughter, and I do not presume to replace him in your heart, but I would not leave you on your own." *Again.* "So long as you wish to come with me, I will gladly have you there. With me." He let his hand fall away and thought; *time to be brave. Again.* "But there are things I have not told you, still, and I…I fear how you might react."

She frowned up at him. "Really? You told me you were in love with my pa and I didn't hate you, but you think there's something else that would make me do so?"

"It is rather complicated."

"I don't care. I want to go with you. Anywhere is better than here. If I end up hating you, then that's that, isn't it? You offered me a job with your landlady, I can take that and ignore you until I've saved up enough to go on my own. I'll be *away* from here. That's all I want."

Lawrence wanted to laugh with joy. "You sound exactly like John."

She flinched, but her eyes were wet and grateful when she looked at him. "Good," she said. "I'm his daughter, after all."

"That you are. Ah, now, what's this?"

Having looked away to give Josephine some privacy, his eyes had fallen on a strange mark in the back of the closet. It was close to the bottom, faint scratches; when he brought the light closer, he could see it better. The numbers *1 2 8*.

"What do you suppose it means?" Josephine asked.

"I've not a clue."

THEY FOUND NOTHING else of import in the room, save a frayed cravat that Henry must have dropped beneath the bed. Lawrence asked Josephine why she had not found it when cleaning the room, but she shrugged and said Richards had done the cleaning in there.

"He said I needed time with my grief, and he'd take care of it," she explained. "He was right. I was sat by the docks crying for hours."

She seemed embarrassed to tell him, yet she still did so; Lawrence took it as a good sign. The moment John had opened up, had been willing to share memories of his low points, was the moment they had truly started to become close.

But none of it lessened his suspicions. Something was wrong in this town, and it seemed the Reverend was at the heart of it. He slept not a wink that night, and when dawn rose (as much as it ever did here), he could feel the exhaustion settling deep in his bones. He could not stay in bed, he knew. He had more mysteries to solve. He needed to clear his head. A walk by the water, perhaps? It would smell awful, but every part of this town did, and the fresh air would do him good.

Whichever parts of the town had woken by now had clearly gone fishing or to other work already—the streets were entirely bereft of life, and Lawrence walked down them alone, until he came to the beach.

Yes, it did smell awful and in the distance he could hear the horrid screams of seagulls. But the air woke him up better than anything else could, and he walked to the ocean's edge to simply look. Despite the murky, gray-green depths, gazing at the water calmed him. It seemed a reminder that there was a world beyond Osmund; he wondered how many of its townsfolk had stood here as he did, dreaming, wondering about a life beyond this shore.

That was when he became aware of a shadow by one of the smaller docks. Standing on the edge of it, staring out over the ocean much as he was, stood a short, hunched-over figure, long black hair whipping in the wind. Lawrence moved closer, feet sinking into the sand; finally, he saw that it was Marie Sinclair, in only her night-gown, hair falling loose down her back, over her face. She had her arms around herself in an embrace, and her head was held low against the wind and salt-spray coming in from the sea.

His first thought was that she should not be out of bed yet, that she was still recovering from the birth. Then, he thought that she should not be out in so little clothes, and were those stains of blood on the stomach of her gown— had she torn her stitches? She should definitely not be out here *alone*, either, not in her state.

Lawrence did not manage to get any more than a few steps closer before Marie walked forward. It was between one moment and the next; Marie hovering in the air, on her way as if simply walking down a path. Then her fall and the water closing over her head, swallowing her whole.

He might have yelled, but his voice was lost to the wind as he attempted to outrun wind and voice both. Lawrence made it up the dock in record time, diving inelegantly into the water. His one coherent thought was that he was not as strong a swimmer as Henry, and was this the dock he had fallen from in his drunken state?

The water was icy cold, piercing his skin like knives. Lawrence almost gasped, but he managed to hold in his breath because he *had to*. He could see Marie below, hair cascading upwards as if reaching for the sky. Her arms were outstretched, eyes closed. Lawrence's eyes stung, but he had to keep them open, had to try and see through the murky waters.

Lawrence had never been a particularly strong man, not when it came to physicality, but in desperation the body found a hitherto unknown reserve. He grasped Marie and pulled, legs kicking as he swum upwards. Everything burned, his arms, his legs, his eyes, but he did not relent. They broke the surface together, her back pressed tightly to his chest. He swum awkwardly backwards, one arm cleaving the water, heading for the shore. He thought he could hear voices, back on the beach, but no one came to help. He hit the sand, grappling for purchase, and then managed to drag her free of the water.

Marie had already started coughing, and he turned her on her side to let the water run free. It spilled from her mouth, greenish, as she hacked until he thought her lungs might burst. The material of the night-gown clung to her, and he could see the outline of the stitches, one of them indeed torn. The trail of blood had merged with the water, painting the dress a faint pink over her stomach.

"Doctor…" she said, voice hoarse, and then coughed again. Lawrence thumped her on the back, helping to hold her steady. Her shoulders were sharp pieces of bone beneath his fingers—she had lost a tremendous amount of weight in a matter of days. She had promised him she was eating, but now he was starting to doubt.

He had thoroughly neglected his patient, and his hands shook with remorse.

"I am so sorry," he said, unable to specify; he was sorry for all of it. "Dear girl, we have to get you inside, get you somewhere warm…"

Her hand interrupted him, his sodden sleeve grasped in an iron grip. "No," she said, water spilling over her lips. "Not home. No, I can't go home."

"But, you…" He took a deep breath. He had dealt with patients both delirious and afraid before. It would not do to start fighting with them. "Of course, we can go to the inn, but you must come with me and lie down. I have to check you over."

She relaxed all at once, slumping into him. Despite feeling his own exhaustion now, Lawrence managed to take both her weight and his own, dragging them to their feet and walking unsteadily and slowly back towards the inn. He made a quick decision to skirt the town square, though it gained them ten steps more, in favor of going behind the inn and coming to the entrance from the other side. His decision seemed to be the right one, as Marie breathed an audible sigh of relief.

Inside the inn was only Josephine, eating her breakfast. Her spoon clattered to the floor when she saw them.

"What…"

"Help me get her upstairs, that's a dear."

It was a relief to have Josephine take some of her weight; despite her small stature, she was strong from a life of manual labor, and between them they got Marie upstairs quickly. She also obeyed his instructions almost before he had time to give them. They stripped Marie of her drenched clothes, scrubbing her harshly with blankets and towels, before Josephine forced one of her own, simple dresses over her head. She shivered through it all, lips tinted blue, but she did not fight them; she was as a doll, movements sluggish and eyes glazed over, staring far away. Lawrence got her piled under covers on the bed, even spreading his coat over her, while Josephine ran downstairs to make hot tea.

He was gently wrapping Marie's hair in a towel, patting it dry, when she spoke:

"You should have let me drown."

He gritted his teeth. "That would be rather against the oath I took."

"What oath is that?" Her voice was so faint, a trembling wisp. He wanted to shush her gently, tell her to get some rest, but her eyes were back in the land of the living now, and he did not wish her to go away too quick again.

"Doctor's swear an oath to help all living beings. I cannot stand by and let someone suffer if I can prevent it."

To his surprise, she snorted, though there was little mirth in the sound. "Should have let me drown," she repeated, and he understood, then, or at least thought he did.

He ran his fingers through her hair gently, untangling the knots. "I can make no concrete promises for the future," he said. "I can only speak from my own experience. You asked me once if I had ever been a parent, and I told you no. That was not a lie, but it was not the whole truth either."

Her eyes grew hazy for a moment, but then she refocused. Still, exhaustion was taking over. He had to speak quickly, before she fell asleep.

"I had a child," he said. "And I lost them. Rather by… rather by my own choice. I held them in my arms once in my life, and that was it. I will not claim to know what you are going through exactly, but I know loss. And I know that the step after, and the step after that, unbearable though they may seem—they will get easier."

Marie's eyes fell closed. "I will never have a child," she said. She sounded, almost, relieved.

"Perhaps not. But you will be alright."

She made a deep sound; she was already asleep. Lawrence gently laid the towel out beneath her head and hair, before standing up from the bed.

A shadow moved in the doorway, and he almost screamed. It was only Josephine, a tray with steaming mugs in her hands.

"Calm down," she told him, with a wry smile on her lips. It faded as she looked at Marie. "I heard you talking. Is she…will she be alright?"

He watched Josephine as she put the tray down on the nightstand, hardly making a sound. An easy, practiced maneuver. "I do not know," he said. "If she recovers physically, then the rest is up to her." He had hope that she would. The torn stitches had not been as bad as he had feared, and he had managed to sew them quickly while Josephine had wrapped her in blankets. Marie had not even seemed to notice, despite that it must have hurt. Shock was a hell of a numbing balm.

Josephine handed him one of the cups. "Drink this. And then change your clothes so you don't get sick either."

"What?"

She shot him an unimpressed look. "Doctor, *you're* still soaked through."

He looked down at himself, at the puddle beneath his feet, at the wet imprint he'd left where he had knelt on the bed. A shiver went through him, and he realized then how damned cold he was. "Oh."

"Yes, oh." Josephine watched as he gulped down the tea. It was almost unbearably hot, the cup against his fingertips and the liquid down his throat. But it sent a shock of warmth through him like an elixir of life; he was not aware how much feeling he had lost in his limbs until it abruptly returned.

"Ah, and…" He looked down at himself again, and then at Josephine, at the sleeping Marie. "Um, I'll just take some clothes and go to…another room."

Josephine rolled her eyes, and turned her back. "Just change already, I've no interest in peeking, old man."

He balked at that; but he still did not move. He had not changed his clothes in the same room as anyone since… since John. He trusted Josephine, but still he kept standing, unable and perhaps unwilling to move. His throat worked, but he did not know what to say, how to explain. It had been seen as eccentricity among his fellows in the city, an all-consuming shyness that did not matter much in the grand scheme of things. But here, with the ever-practical Josephine, his aversion seemed a much bigger beast, a silly thing of misplaced propriety and city-manners.

"You're not breathing," Josephine observed, still with her back to him. She dared peek over her shoulder, well-knowing that he had not moved at all. "Do you…did I break you, doctor?" Still, he did not answer. "Oh, shit."

"Language!"

"Now you speak." She turned to him fully. "Look, it's alright, I'll step outside."

Marie would still be in here. But she was buried beneath piles of blankets, fast asleep. Josephine gently closed the door shut behind her, and a shiver traveled through Lawrence. He really was damned cold.

He opened the closet, managing to angle the doors of it so it would be even more difficult to see him from the bed (just in case Marie did wake up) and then he changed as quickly as possible, grabbing the first articles of clothing he could see. His bags were still only half unpacked, and the shirt he found was severely wrinkled—he could just imagine Mrs. Danson's outrage at seeing him wear it in such a state. He did not care. He peeled the damp clothing away, breathing deep as he got rid of socks and unwrapped heavy bandages, and quickly grabbed another shirt to wipe himself down with.

When he was finished and fully dressed, he walked over to open the door. Josephine was sitting on the floor out there, her back to the wall.

"You done being weird?"

He could not help but flush. "It is not weird to have manners. What if someone had walked in, me half-naked and two unchaperoned women in my room?" *One in my bed, even.*

"You're a *doctor.* Aren't you supposed to not care about nudity?" As she stood up, he realized she was not actually questioning him—only teasing. His shoulders fell in relief.

They walked back inside, and Lawrence dragged the desk-chair over to the bed, while Josephine perched on the edge of the mattress. Marie's breathing was slow, but color had already returned to her lips, a flush on her cheeks that could mean either fever or renewed life.

Lawrence sagged, the power of shock and action leaving his body. He rested his face in his hands, breathing deep.

"It's alright, doctor. You saved her."

He could have easily been too late. If he had not gone down to the beach at all, Marie would be deep below now, void of life.

They sat in silence for a moment, before it seemed too much for Josephine.

"I didn't mean to eavesdrop, but you know I heard you two talking. You said you'd had a child?"

Oh, he was glad she could not see his face just then. Lawrence forced himself to keep breathing. Then he lowered his hands.

"Yes."

Josephine would not meet his eyes. "Want to tell me about it?"

"One day."

She didn't seem pleased with that answer, but from her darting eyes he guessed that she'd expected him to deny it or tell her it was none of her business. She changed the subject:

"Why did you bring her here?"

He tensed, remembering. "She said not to take her home. She seemed afraid."

Their eyes met. "Thompson," Josephine said. "He's been there a lot lately." She slid off the bed. "I'll go ask Marlyn about it."

Lawrence wasn't sure what Marlyn would know, but then again, he had seen the two men speaking a few times. Or rather, Marlyn had spoken. He did not think he had ever heard a single word pass Thompson's lips.

"Be careful," he told her. He should have insisted she not go alone, but there was something about her competency that relaxed him. That, and he could not in good conscience leave his patient alone right now. "Come right back here after you've talked with him."

"I will." She reached out a hand, as if on instinct, before catching herself. It hovered in the space between them; she had, Lawrence realized, been reaching out as if to touch his shoulder.

He wanted to tell her that she could. That he would wrap her up in a father's hug, if he could. That she was safe here, that she need not hesitate.

Her hand dropped. He said nothing. The door clicked gently closed behind her.

HE WOKE MARIE to have her drink some tepid tea. She was still shivering, but her eyes were less glassy, her cheeks still rosy. He rearranged the blankets around her, tucking her in tighter—she fell asleep mid-sentence, promising him she felt better. He checked her stitches, her temperature. He paced along the floor.

He almost tripped over the huge ledger still lying there. Ah, right—he had forgotten all about that. He picked it up, resting it half on the bed as he sat down.

On a whim, he counted to page 128; but there seemed to be nothing of interest. Two stillbirths, a drowning, three successful births, though one had died ten years later as he fell from the roof of the church in a silly game with the other boys in town.

He sighed and started over from the beginning. He could quickly skip those pages again, reading over those born decades before. There, fifty-eight years ago: the birth of *William Thompson*. Lawrence's fingers hovered over the name, as if he could discern the man's secrets by touch alone.

There was a note, dates and page-numbers beneath his name. A wedding, he realized, and two births.

He flipped to those pages, finding the birth-date of *Auma Thompson, nee Moran*, married to William thirty-six years ago. There was a death-date with her name. The cause was listed in steady letters: *Suicide*.

A terrible feeling rose in Lawrence as he flicked ahead to the first page indicated under both their names. *Firstborn son of William and Auma Thompson*. There, clearly on the page—born twenty-four years ago. *Marlyn William Thompson*.

It really was not good for a surgeon's hands to shake as much as they had been doing recently. As if in a dream, Lawrence turned to the last page. A sister. *Katherine Louise Thompson*. Born nineteen years ago. Died six years ago. No cause of death was listed, though Richards had told him of the bloody body on the stairs of the church. There was merely the cross and year, indicating a passing, followed by a stark *X* written at the end of the entry.

The book slipped from his hands and landed on the floor with a dull thud. Marie mumbled in her sleep. Lawrence barely heard it over the pounding of his own heart.

Killed by a mob, Richards had told him. The murderer of his own daughter, murdered by the denizens of the town. Except he was still walking free, out in the open, as clearly evidenced by the ledger. A ledger Richards had freely handed him, with a smile. Unless this was a different Thompson? But William's brothers had all died young. There was no other Thompson's listed—just the two of them. Marlyn and William.

Did that mean the Reverend truly did not know what was going on here? Why would he so readily hand over evidence to Lawrence while lying right to his face? Did he not know the truth either, somehow?

Was it Thompson, then? Who was behind it all? And… and Marlyn. Who was seemingly grieving his lost sister, but what, was still drinking beer with the man who had killed her?

Horror struck him to the core, just as he reached down for the book. Marlyn could be in on it. Marlyn, who he had just sent Josephine to go talk to. Alone.

He was out of the door like a shot, clutching the ledger to his chest (it was *evidence!*). Quickly, quickly. He made it outside, not even noticing how cold it was without his coat. Where did Marlyn live? Richards had pointed it out to him, when he had briefly shown him around town, but Lawrence had not paid that much attention, certain that he would not be staying long. Such a fool he had been.

There, he was sure it was there, a shack more than a house, paint that had once been blue chipping away under the force of the wind. He all but crashed into the door, relieved when it swung open with little resistance, though it did make his shoulder smart.

Josephine was not inside, nor was Marlyn. Instead he found Thompson standing there, in the unlit room, a pool of shadows at his feet and a startled expression on his weathered face.

It was not a pool of shadows, Lawrence realized, at the same time as Thompson's face turned from surprised to murderous. It was his coat, which he had shed for the first time since Lawrence had seen him, lying at his feet.

The body it had hidden Lawrence could best describe as *mangled*. Long scars crossed his torso, crawling over his belly and around to his back. His arms and shoulders were in a like state. Slashes, stitches, stabs—all of them decorated William Thompson's body like a tapestry of horror.

The few places of his body untouched by scarring were almost as misshapen; parts of skin either irritated pink or dull gray, other parts flaking off like the paint outside.

Worst were the fresh-looking scars over his chest, a bad, clumsy carving of a tree that Lawrence had become very familiar with. He almost missed the carving of a long-fingered hand holding a cup, placed lower on the side of his belly. It was fresh enough to still be bleeding lightly.

Lawrence stood frozen in terror, as Thompson reached down and, with a strange, gentle air, pulled his coat back over his shoulders, obscuring his nightmare of a torso. "Well," he said, and that was almost as shocking as the sight, the fact that this man spoke, with a voice low and gravelly, but unmistakably human. "Guess I'll have to kill you now."

L ATER, LAWRENCE WOULD not be able to remember what had happened. There was the moment when Thompson lunged at him, and then there was the moment Lawrence woke up in bed, bruised and battered. Everything in-between was a dark void.

It was Josephine, sitting vigilant at his bedside, who told him what had happened—or at least, what they assumed had happened, before anyone else arrived on the scene. Thompson had made to kill him, had gotten his hands around his throat, squeezing the life out of him—he had the marks on his throat to prove it, broad fingers imprinted—when Marlyn had arrived at the scene and knocked Thompson over the head. That sounded believable enough; what Lawrence had a hard time imagining was that, after the blow had made Thompson release him, though it had not knocked him out, Lawrence had managed to beat him back, knocking him into a table.

The commotion of that had drawn others, but in the hubbub, no one quite knew what had happened, not even Marlyn. Lawrence had been knocked down, as Thompson leapt for him again—a rather violent blow to the head had knocked him out; Lawrence would later reach up numb fingers and prod at the bulge on the back of his head, wincing in pain.

Thompson had been about to finish him off when a gunshot had rung out, alerting the rest of the town.

Marlyn had shot his father. Right between the eyes, if Josephine was to be believed. The corpse had already been dragged off to the undertaker.

None of it made sense to Lawrence's sore head. He fell asleep again, at some point, only to wake up later, Josephine asleep sitting in the chair, her head resting on the edge of the mattress.

He gently touched her hair to wake her. "Josephine."

Her head rose slowly. "Yeah? Pa…oh, doctor. Hi."

"You can call me Lawrence." He had said so before, but she seemed to prefer the other moniker.

"What?"

"I am in my room," he said instead, because indeed he was; he recognized the dresser, the writing desk. "Where is Marie?"

"We don't know. No-one's seen her."

There was a painful clenching in his chest. No doubt she had gone to finish the task he had thwarted. He thought of Auma, Marlyn's and Kya's mother, deep below the waves. The sea had claimed Henry, too. The churning sea, eating people and spitting out corpses. He closed his eyes again.

He slept intermittently, waking to Josephine's steady presence, and once to the Reverend as well, saying prayers. Lawrence did not recognize the Latin spoken, but his head was muddled, and he had never been much interested in the Biblical parts of the language. Not when there were names of medicine and illnesses to memorize. He had, thankfully, not stayed awake long while Richards was there.

At one point he awoke, sweat on his brow and his chest heaving, with the realization that someone must have undressed him earlier to check for injuries. Someone…but he had not been decried or asked, and even in his panic, exhaustion soon pulled him back to sleep. By the time he woke up again, he endeavored to mention nothing unless directly confronted.

When they were alone, and when Lawrence was a bit more alert, he recounted to Josephine what he had learned.

"I didn't know," she said. "About Marlyn, not any of it. Should we ask…"

"We don't know who to trust," he said. "Perhaps Thompson had this town in a grip of terror and that is why no-one spoke plainly." Something unfurled in his chest—it was relief. Perhaps this was all over? It did seem as if the sun shone just a bit brighter outside, though it hardly shone at all. It could be his head injury. "I think," he said. "I think when I am recovered, we are leaving. It is time."

His eyes slipped closed on Josephine's relieved face.

XVIII.

H E WOKE IN the night to footsteps. The window was opened, though he could not recall it being so when he had fallen asleep. He raised his head from the pillow, muttering a *hello?* The dark drapes floated in the wind. There was no-one there.

Lawrence would later blame it on the head injury; the fact that he looked up and saw Marie, long dark hair mingling with her black dress.

The white drapes fluttered around Marie as she darted out the window; she was long gone by the time Lawrence's shouting had roused the others and made them come running to his side.

"I am sure it was just a nightmare," Richards said, kindly. His teeth gleamed in the moonlight. Josephine double-checked that the window was secure; Marlyn was there too, he realized with a start, but the man would not look at him. He had not thanked him for saving his life, and right then Lawrence found that he could not—that he almost did not want to.

"I'll stay in here for the night," Josephine said.

"Oh, please, I know you were looking forward to your own bed…"

"It was not a suggestion," she said, and he almost laughed, at how much he felt like a child, and she the parent.

They were left alone, and soon as the door closed, Josephine climbed into the bed, on top of his covers, wrapped in one of his blankets.

"I hope you don't mind," she said. "I'm tired."

She laid with her back to him. Outside, in the hallway, the wood creaked beneath someone's feet. People were settling back into sleep. It occurred to him that her comfort with him had reached levels it would usually take years to accomplish between two people. It could be because she had stayed here, nursed him back to health. It could be because he had shared a secret with her.

Not the biggest one, though.

"Josephine."

"Hm?"

"Are you awake?"

"Wouldn't be talking if I weren't."

"Some people talk in their sleep." He was being nonsensical. He was stalling.

"Sure." Neither of them said that John had, but Lawrence guessed they were both thinking it.

"It occurred to me," he said, slowly. He was sweating, but he did not dare move to adjust the covers. "That when I woke here, in bed, I…well, I was wearing my clothes, but I thought…"

"I checked you over for injuries," she said. "But it was just your throat and head. Do you—are you feeling pain somewhere else? Are you alright?"

"I am, I am, do not fret. Josephine, I was only wondering whether anyone had looked beneath my clothes while I was out of it."

"Are you worried about your modesty right now?"

"Never," he mocked, just to hear her laugh. "No, I was only wondering."

"Don't worry, I've been guarding you. Your virtue is intact."

"Good, good." If she had seen, that might have made this conversation easier. He was infinitely glad she hadn't, though, that the decision was still in his hands. That he had not been robbed of his privacy, necessary as it might have been. "It is only that I have something to tell you."

She turned, but only to her back, so that they were both lying with their eyes pointed to the ceiling, shoulder to shoulder. She waited. As the silence stretched out, she kept waiting, though he felt her eyes briefly turn to him, before they returned to the wooden planks above.

"I am…that is to say…" Oh, the last time he had done this, he had been so very drunk. Perhaps he should ask her to fetch some of that wine. "That is to say, had you seen, had I been otherwise injured, you might have seen… that, I suppose…well, that there are certain similarities, between you and me."

He could almost hear her frowning. "In…what way?"

"Anatomically."

The silence alone might make him vomit.

"I don't know…"

"Ah, of course. Anatomy is the, um, study of the body… that is to say, the human body…what I am trying to say, is…" He was turning into a puddle of sweat and nerves. The covers were suffocating, but he still dared not move. He was infinitely grateful that Josephine was not looking at him. "It is to say that I, that my body, is rather more like yours than it is like, say, Henry's. Or Marlyn's. Or… that is to say…I-I picked the name Lawrence for myself, when I was very young, and then my uncle helped me with…it is a big world out there, Josephine, and there are all sorts of people…" He was ranting. He had to stop.

Lawrence took a deep breath, closed his eyes. "I loved John very much. He loved me back, and he accepted me for who and what I was, in a way no one ever had before. Body and spirit both."

Seconds ticked into minutes. He wished to keep talking, to fill the silence, to make Josephine understand, but he recognized this silence; John had lived in it, too, when he had first told him. She was putting things together, thinking it over. Trying, he realized, to understand. Perhaps failing to understand at all. He had to give her time.

Finally, she spoke. "Women can't be doctors," she said. "They aren't allowed to."

"Quite. But I am not a woman. Despite what some might say." The truth of it coated his tongue—panic gave way to a giddy feeling. It was out, it was out now, the first part done. Time to throw himself recklessly into the next. "I always meant to tell you this," he said. "Since I invited you to come with me."

"You've told others?"

"Your father, of course. And Henry knew."

Josephine turned her head to look at him. "You aren't a woman?"

"No."

"You just…have the body of one."

"If you would like to phrase it that way."

He could not see her eyes properly, though the white of them stood out. He was glad he had done it like this, that the darkness covered him; but he hated it too, that he could not watch her face freely. See the truth of her feelings.

"I don't know if I understand," she said. "But I…I don't know. Your name is Lawrence?"

"It has been for many years now."

"Then…" She sighed, slumping back against the bed. "This is very confusing, but you've been confusing since I met you."

"Oh, thank you."

She laughed. "What a secret! Is that all of it, now?"

He thought he might vomit, or perhaps start laughing. Either way, best not to open his mouth right now.

Josephine's own laughter faded. "It's not, is it?"

"I have no excuse," he said. "I have nothing I can offer you save a sincere apology, and an explanation. I had a deep desire to keep the life I had fought so hard to carve out for myself. Yet John wanted to be a father, or at least he found he wished for that when I became… that is to say…when we discovered I was pregnant. It was something I could do for him, keep it, and when it all came down to it, I did not hate the state as much as I thought I would, the whole process of it. But it was easier, to part ways, to have him keep you and for you to be happy, because otherwise what might people have thought? We were worried, about rumors, about what might be found out. How it would affect not just ours, but your life as well. And I did not wish to…I did not want a child of my own, not to raise. Not at the time." He had gotten older since then, had known a new kind of loneliness. He had met Josephine, now. "Had I known when he died, I would have…provided for you, of course. I never meant for…we agreed, to keep separate entirely. Agreed that it was easier. For your sake. I only wanted the best for you, and that was not me. I could not be your mother, and you already had a father, one who would do anything for you. It was better that way."

He took a deep breath, his throat dry. Josephine seemed to not be breathing, so still was she. "I understand this might be too much altogether. I have no expectations of you. I have no claim over you. Just know that I…that despite what you might think of me now, I am very glad to have met you. And whatever you should require of me, I will gladly give it. Be that distance or money or…or family."

Lawrence felt light-headed. He felt giddy, he felt, already, filled with such grief, as if Josephine had died in front of him.

Slowly, she rose from the bed. "I am going to go sleep in my room," she said, with no emotion in her voice.

Lawrence could not feel his body; even had he wanted to, he could not move or speak. He did not look at her as she left the bed, leaving the blanket behind. She walked to the door, twisting the knob—they had not locked it, too tired, too preoccupied with the window. Lawrence could only see her out of the corner of his eye; so he did not understand why she opened the door, but did not go through it, instead staring into the shadows of the hallway. Slowly, Josephine shook her head, though at who or what, Lawrence could not tell.

Not until the shadows moved, and Marlyn appeared from them to yank her towards him, his face pale, eyes wide. Josephine yelled, her voice pitched with anger and Lawrence jumped from the bed, ignoring the pain that shot through his body.

Marlyn clasped a hand over Josephine's mouth, struggling with her as she twisted and clawed at him. "Reverend!" he shouted. "Rev, it's him—stop fighting me! Josephine!"

Lawrence did not understand, and he understood even less when Josephine seemed to obey, but he did not care to in that moment. Whatever had given him strength when he had seen Marie walk into the water seized him again now. All he could think was that he had to get her free, had to make Marlyn stop, had to get them out of here. Had to get her safe.

He was not prepared for Thompson to step out of the shadows too. Fear shot through him, overriding everything else, and he nearly stumbled—the monstrous man grasped him, fingers finding their place around his throat once more. They squeezed; his vision blackened.

"Now, now, William," Reverend Richards' voice came from somewhere behind him. "Be not too harsh with the good Doctor. I'd like for him to stay alert for the next part."

It was the last thing Lawrence heard before everything went dark.

LAWRENCE WOKE UP in the church. Or rather, he thought he woke up—if someone had told him just then that he was, in fact, very dead, he would believe them. Except he did not think death was supposed to *hurt* this much. His chest felt as if an elephant had stepped on it, and his throat had been set on fire. It hurt more than his head, at least, though his vision swam when he opened his eyes.

What he saw did not help. He was in the church, no doubt, but the pews had been pushed aside to make space. Candles stood everywhere, on the floor, up the few steps to the presbytery, precariously close to where Lawrence's legs stretched out in front of him. His hands had been bound, and he was propped up against one of the pews.

Red paint covered the floor, strange symbols drawn in an elaborate, swirling pattern—Lawrence did not recognize a single one of them, but the sight sent shivers down his spine. Several circles of the symbols ringed each other, growing smaller until they reached the middle where—oh, there was Josephine, awake but bound as well, her jaw set in defiance, her cheek swollen from a blow. She was looking right at him with tears in her eyes—and relief, too, when he looked back at her. And then anger—but not at him.

He rather thought it was directed at Richards, who stood above her. The Reverend wore a long, dark robe, one far more suited for some theatrical performance than whatever this was. He looked taller than he ever had before, and the smile on his face seemed a permanent fixture now, as if someone had carved it into his skin. Marlyn was there as well, standing at the edge of the first circle; and next to Lawrence stood Thompson, twice-dead and still breathing.

"Ah, you're awake," Richards turned to stare at him. There was a book in his hand, old and tattered, the cover fraying in his hands. He held it reverently, as if it was some holy icon. "Good. I wanted to thank you in person. And also to tell you how much of an *idiot* you are!"

Lawrence was barely listening. His eyes met Josephine's. They were angry, but wide with fear as well. He felt it course through him, as if she had transferred her emotions. If he could take her fear, he would. If he could do anything, he would.

"This is unnecessary," Thompson said, his voice too-loud in the echo of the church. Richards' eyes were wide, bloodshot. A muscle jumped in his cheek.

"Oh, it is *very* necessary. For my pleasure if nothing else." Everything about him was bloodless as he stood in the glow of the candles, and though he did not move, it seemed to Lawrence that he was suddenly closer. "You are the most *infuriating* person I have ever had the misfortune to meet! All those clues missed, all that *time* you took to just dawdle! All you had to do was *confirm* who you were to Josephine, and we could have been done so much sooner!"

Lawrence's throat could produce little more than a croak, but he managed to get the words out somehow: "I don't understand."

"No, of course you don't! Imbecile! All those breadcrumbs I spread for you, and you barely followed a one! You dug up the corpse immediately, and I was so pleased, and then just *nothing*! You could have checked the wine-cellar, man! Right beneath the church!" He stamped one foot, as if to emphasize his point. "And then you almost left right away, and we had to set poor Sinclair to giving birth ahead of time, just to have you stay! But still you just proved *awful* at this. Did you even find the carving beneath your bed? The secret cove? The letters in the attic? The numbers in the Bible? In the closet? Did you even notice that William had your friend's old pipe? No, of course you didn't! You're a half-brain! How you made it through medical school is a mystery to me!"

"I don't...why would you..."

Richards composed himself. He was still smiling—had not stopped smiling, even as his eyes had alighted with anger during his angry spiel. "To make you *stay*! I had to be sure—all those times gone wrong." He sighed. "*Poor* Marie's daughter had to let her life, because despite what the good Bard says, a child ripped from the womb is *not* a proper fulfillment of the requirements."

"*What* requirements?" Josephine snapped. Richards' reached down to pat the top of her head, clearly pleased with the question. He had to quickly withdraw when she snapped at his fingers, her teeth clicking together on empty air.

"There, now, don't be mean. I understand you simpletons are unfamiliar with the Good Word, of course. I will try to be patient—it is a virtue, after all."

He gingerly moved a page of the book, though his eyes did not leave Lawrence's face. "I have been trying for years to bring Him to earth. To be the vessel He requires." Another muscle twitched in his face—no, Lawrence realized, it was not a muscle. Something was moving, beneath his skin, something alive. "There is one last piece I need, and nothing and none seemed to fit. As if such a thing didn't exist. I had all but given up when dear Berkeley arrived. When he *recognized* Josephine. He was easy, you know, to get all distracted, to lead on his merry way towards mystery and adventure. He appreciated a good clue, unlike the two of you! It was all theory to him, of course, but a theory he was eager to prove reality. He started to believe when he realized I couldn't sign my own name, of course. And he put together that the clues meant nothing, too—oh, but he was so fun to distract. And by then he had told me what I wanted to know, had spilled your secrets quite easily."

"I don't believe that," Lawrence said, even as his heart wrenched with the thought of betrayal.

"Fine, he was severely drugged before he told me that you might have given birth to little Josephine here. Truly, I was just going to try the ritual right away, but Thompson insisted we needed confirmation." Richards looked to the side, directing that smile at the other man. "Sick of the senseless killing, weren't you? But nothing is senseless. Not for Our Lord. He will rise…"

"Reverend," Marlyn said, eyes flickering back and forth. "Please just…get it over with."

"Wait," Lawrence pleaded. His wrists were chafed raw trying to break free from the ropes, but he'd made no progress. He needed more time. "Wait, please, wait. I—I…so what was one-hundred and twenty-eight? What did it mean?"

Richards snorted. "Page 128 in the fine collection of Shakespeare's works that I left in your room. It says much the same there as it does here." He tapped a finger gently against a page in his book. "I doubt the old Bard of Avon had read the Book of Him, though. Perhaps he got the idea elsewhere. But he misinterpreted it, just as I did."

"Just *tell* us," Josephine hissed. Lawrence could see her shoulders straining, but she was bound fast too, unable to escape.

"Allow me to translate. To summon He Who Never Drowns in Shadow—not a direct translation of his name, but rather poetic, don't you think? I came up with it myself. Anyway," he continued, when it seemed no one in his audience was going to applaud. "The ritual requires a sacrifice, a human bled out by His altar. But the human must be *none of woman born*. Do you understand? Do you see?"

A hysterical laugh bubbled up in Lawrence's throat. "You…you…"

"Yes. I could not imagine what perverse creature it could refer to. I tried orphans. I tried those cut from the womb, like Macduff in the play. I tried the babes born of those not *quite* there—it was a shame, of course, with little Kya, but it had to be tried, and Auma proved herself true to the diagnosis when she let the sea take her."

Lawrence saw movement out of the corner of his eye: it was Marlyn taking a single step forward before stopping. His jaw was slack with dumb shock. Had this, then, been the first he knew of what had really happened to Kya? Behind him Thompson stood still and unmovable as a statue. Lawrence could see the stark white of his eyes shining in the dark.

Richards continued: "None of it mattered. I was ready to give up entirely. And then I was told of *you*, dear doctor. And the child you'd had, who'd already found her way to me. Providence, faith." His eyes rolled up, raised towards the sky. "Destiny."

"You sick *fuck*," Josephine said, though she was not looking at Richards or even Thompson, but at Marlyn.

"You let them kill her! And you…*fuck* this town!"

Marlyn flinched and looked away, turning his head as if he could hide from it all if only he stopped looking.

"Now, now," Richards said. "No profanity in the house of our Lord."

"Fuck you," said Lawrence.

Richards tutted. "Truly. I understand you're upset, now, but this is your last opportunity to have your questions answered. I will be killing you both in a minute or so."

Josephine lunged, but she was easily kicked back by Richards. She lost her balance, tumbling the rest of the way to the floor. There were tears and red paint streaking her face when she lifted her eyes again, looking at Lawrence. No, he could not let her die. He would not.

"I have a question," he said, scrambling for one even as he said it. "I…how can you be sure?"

"Of?"

"Of me. That I am telling the truth."

"What a tale to make up if it isn't true!"

"And yet…yet all you have is Marlyn's word for it, do you not? He's been spying on us all this time." By the grave, in the kitchen. Outside their door. When else had he been there? He must have dogged their every step. "And Marlyn has every reason to hate you."

Richards laughed. "You think I doubt the loyalty of my men? Most of the town knows what goes on here, knows not to cross me. William watched his own daughter bleed out, by my word. Everyone knew who he was, hated him for his loyalty to me, yet none dared raise a hand against him. How many times have we faked your death now, William? At least thrice. Marlyn has been ever so helpful with that."

Thompson winced. Marlyn turned his head to look at his father, lips trembling. He seemed shocked, but he did not move. Lawrence grasped at that like a starving man for bread. "They've never done the least thing to make you doubt them?" Stalling, stalling, he had to get more time, though he had no plan, nothing he could do.

There, a flicker in Richards' eyes, though his smile never lessened. "William does have a soft heart." He said, of the murderer. "He is rather fond of taking my sacrifices out early if they prove insufficient. But it is not a flaw to wish mercy upon others. In fact, I rather like him for it." He twitched—there it was again, something crawling, undulating under his skin—moving from his face down his neck. "Ah, We are getting impatient. No more questions, dear doctor. It is time."

No, no, no. Lawrence's throat closed up as Richards moved the book to one hand, drawing a dagger from the folds of his robe with the other. Marlyn stepped forward; he hesitated again, but at a look from the Reverend, he grabbed Josephine's hair, pulling her head back. Baring her throat.

No, no, no. Lawrence was only half-aware that he was saying it out loud. He thought he might choke on the sound. He scrambled to move forwards, but Thompson grabbed his shoulder, keeping him easily in place. Weak, he was too weak. He would not be able to save her. He *had* to. He struggled, enough that Thompson had to get closer, and then he pushed, trying to topple him to the floor; but the other man was a mountain, unmovable.

"Please," Lawrence said, voice rising. "Please, please, don't do this, please, take me instead..."

"Unfortunately, Lawrence," said Richards. "You do not meet the requirements."

The dagger touched Josephine's throat—Lawrence thought he saw the blood, welling up; he forced himself to keep his eyes open though he wished nothing more than to look away. He thought he saw it, the horrible slash, the gushing of blood. But it was his own mind getting ahead of himself; the blade barely touched her skin before Josephine had pulled away, the back of her head smashing against Marlyn's leg.

"Ow!" Marlyn's grip on her was loose and reluctant. His hands were shaking.

"Marlyn, I said *hold her*, what is this…"

The door to the church opened. Everyone froze, like children caught stealing cookies. What a scene they made, Lawrence thought, and then his mind went blank as Marie Sinclair walked inside.

Her steps were steady and sure, her long dark hair falling down over her shoulders, eyes shining, face pale. She wore his coat, the one he had placed over her sleeping form to keep her warm. *Ah, that's where my journal's gone,* he thought, happy to not have lost it, and then almost laughed at how ridiculous that was. She walked with her hands thrust into the pockets, but though she still shivered from the cold, she seemed confident nonetheless.

Her appearance shocked even Richards; the smile had finally slipped from his face, his mouth instead forming a little *o* of surprise.

She passed through the first circle, then the next; she was barefoot, he noticed, trailing bloody footsteps behind her. No one stopped her, though Richards startled when she came closer, when her hands slipped free of the pockets.

"Don't mind me," she said, and buried a knife in his heart.

IT WAS LAWRENCE'S knife, of course. Marie would return it to him later, when the blade had been cleaned of red and blackish blood, when they were clear of Osmund, when it was all finally over. Or, as over as it could be. The sound Richards had made when the blade had pierced his skin would haunt Lawrence forever.

There had been swearing, and someone screaming. The screaming might have been Lawrence. Josephine, with her hands bound behind her back, had managed to knock Marlyn off his feet. Richards had crumbled to the floor; Marie had not stabbed him only once. She had kept at it, until whatever lived beneath his skin had burst free and almost made her drop the knife.

It was Thompson who had pulled her clear, after freeing Lawrence from his own bonds. He had run to wrench Josephine away from the writhing mass of limbs and blood. When He—when it—when *something* had reached out to snake around Josephine's ankle, to pull her back into danger, Marlyn had yanked her free.

And then Thompson, blood flowing from scars old as the church, had grappled with the thing, knocking over candles until they caught in the wood of the pews, in the long robes. He had said nothing, only looked once at his son, and Marlyn had understood. He'd grabbed a lantern and smashed it on the floor, feeding the flames.

"Go!" he'd shouted, and they had, Lawrence all but carrying Josephine outside, too afraid to let go of her. He thought Marie had dragged Marlyn after them, or perhaps he had run after of his own will. In any case, the four of them made it outside as the fire spread and seemed to grow to an inferno with unnatural speed. The stained glass-windows exploded, the boards caught on fire, the roof started to collapse, caving in on itself as if wanting to make sure the fire would have fuel.

The town of Osmund gathered to watch. Not a one went to fetch water or run inside to save the souls still in there. It did not rain—for once, the weather was mild. Pleasant.

Lawrence would yank at rope until Josephine was free, and then he would find a water-barrel and clean soot from both their faces. Marie would hand him back his coat; she would keep the knife a little longer. Marlyn would trail after them, eyes vacant, a trail of blisters from the fire down one side of his face. No one would stop them or ask what had happened. The townsfolk would watch the church burn, until there was nothing but a hollow skeleton of wood and stone left, and then they would disperse, going back to their homes. The fire would go out with a soft sigh—it had touched nothing else, not even the grass below.

"Can we leave now?" Josephine had asked. "Right now?"

They had packed their bags, all four of them. Lawrence would not have made the decision to bring Marlyn along, but Marie had already stopped him from walking away several times, and he figured she was owed this decision.

The invitation had been extended to her easily, though Lawrence was not sure what Mrs. Danson would say when he came home with three people in tow.

They ended up having to wait for a carriage to ride through, but none of them wished to stay in the town. And so, battered and bruised, they ended up sitting on the dry, yellow grass by the road, waiting as the sun rose and the wind blew over the sea. It was here that Marie had told him of waking in the empty room, of feeling the shape of the knife in the pocket of the coat thrown over her. Of thinking that if she was not going to die, then the man responsible for all of this would.

"He has always been here," she told Lawrence. "For as long as I can remember. When I was a little girl I thought he was kind. He would always let us play outside the church. When he said my husband died at sea, I didn't question it. I saw my husband inside the church as it burned, before you pulled me out. He wore a crown of crab's pincers and carried a spear of carved anemones. He told me *get out of here*. I promised to feed the Reverend to the sea, for him."

"He has been fed to the flames," Lawrence said to her, and then, because he felt savage and grim in that moment, he said: "He suffered, Marie. You can be sure of that."

He would have done more to reassure her, but he was distracted by Josephine sitting close to him. She was shivering and staring right ahead. Even when he looked at her, she did not look back, though it was apparent from her flickering eyes that she was fighting the urge to.

He wanted to ask her what was wrong, but that would be a stupid question considering all that had happened. He wanted to comfort her, but doubt tied itself around him like chains.

"Josephine." He had meant to say more, to inquire after her state, but his mouth refused to shape the words.

She did not turn to look at him, but she did speak.

"I'm sorry. I...I listened to him." There was no need for Lawrence to ask who she was referring to. He thought of her standing by the open door to his room, shaking her head at the shadows. She had not been surprised to see Marlyn there. Only regretful. And then they had both been taken.

"He said I should be careful. He sounded so worried. Did I really know you at all and could I trust that you wanted the best for me? I never trusted him, but I didn't know you..."

"It is alright," Lawrence said. He wished she would look at him and see that he was sincere. "There is nothing to forgive. I understand."

She did not turn his head or speak, but slowly he could feel her arm pressing against his as she leaned up against him, a gradual warmth and weight that broke through the chill in the air.

Josephine fell asleep on his shoulder shortly after. He did not wake her until the carriage arrived, not even when his arm went numb. They would talk, the evening after they had made it back to his house, speak quietly and privately, of the past and of the future. For now, it was enough that she was there, a small nick on her throat reminding them both that she was still alive.

Two days later, at home in the city, and Osmund was starting to feel like a dream. Four days, and he woke up to Marlyn and Marie having left.

"The young lady wanted to thank you," Mrs. Danson explained. "But she said not to wake you. I am afraid she didn't say where they were headed."

"I think Mrs. Sinclair knows what she is doing. I wish them well." Whatever might come next for them.

Josephine was awake and putting sugar cubes in her tea, at least until Mrs. Danson interrupted to do it for her.

Though not well pleased that he'd brought company home without warning her first, Mrs. Danson had been kind to them all; Josephine in particular. She seemed to have picked up on something, because she treated the girl exactly as Lawrence would have expected her to, had he told her she was family.

That is my daughter, he thought, sitting down at the table across from her. The day before, Josephine had fallen asleep in the garden outside, lying under the afternoon sun—freckles had exploded across her darkening skin, and her hair had gone two shades lighter. She looked like John. She looked like him. *Mrs. Danson, this is my daughter, Josephine,* he imagined himself saying and he wanted to laugh and laugh with the joy of it; even if he did not say it out loud, even if he *never* said it out loud, except to himself and to her. It was still true.

She took as much sugar in her tea as he did. Just the right amount, he thought, as Mrs. Danson poured a cup for him too.

About the Author

Nikoline Kaiser is a Danish author with a degree in Comparative Literature from Aarhus University. Her works appear in several journals and publications, including *Strange Horizons, Underland Arcana,* and the Danish *Slagtryk.* In 2023 she was longlisted for the Lee Smith Novel Prize. You can find her on Instagram and bluesky @nikolinekaiser or on her website: nikolinekaiser.dk

About the Press

Neon Hemlock is a Washington, DC-based small press publishing speculative fiction, rad zines, and queer chapbooks. Publishers Weekly once called us "the apex of queer speculative fiction publishing" and we're still beaming. Learn more about us at neonhemlock.com and on social medias at @neonhemlock.

www.ingramcontent.com/pod-product-compliance
Lightning Source LLC
Chambersburg PA
CBHW030942310726
48969CB00008B/2343